Ravenwood
A Novel

Ravenwood
A Novel

story and photos by
Sylvia Spicer

iUniverse, Inc.
Bloomington

Ravenwood
Journey to the Fifth Season

iUniverse books may be ordered through booksellers or by contacting:

iUniverse
1663 Liberty Drive
Bloomington, IN 47403
www.iuniverse.com
1-800-Authors (1-800-288-4677)

ISBN: 978-1-4759-3477-9 (sc)
ISBN: 978-1-4759-3479-3 (hc)
ISBN: 978-1-4759-3478-6 (e)

Printed in the United States of America

iUniverse rev. date: 09/14/2012

Contents

Prologue

Soon after moving to the wilderness of the Pacific Northwest, I allotted time each day to quietly observe nature. Seated on the log of a fallen cedar at the edge of the forest, I was gradually introduced to the wildlife of the area as each animal approached me closely enough to satisfy its curiosity. Before long, I came to know them as individuals with their own qualities, lives, and stories.

Often, the deer were accompanied by a black-and-white cat who appeared perfectly at ease walking in a serpentine fashion among their legs as they grazed. On the ground around the deer herd were ravens, squirrels, chipmunks, and quail. The cat was too involved with what appeared to be conversations with the deer to show any interest in hunting the available prey.

In awe, I observed these routine visits of the forest animals for several weeks until I felt compelled to question the cat, who called himself Topper. One day as he leaned against my leg to clean his fur, I asked how he came to live so amicably among these animals. Each day

I asked new questions of him, and in each remarkable response I found enlightenment.

For years the cat answered my questions, yet only ever asked one question of me: "Who are you?" Topper was not like any other cat I had ever known. His stories helped me to understand that the answer to his one question depended on the values that govern one's life.

Ravenwood is a compilation of his stories (as I interpreted them) relating to his home in the mountains and forests of the Pacific Northwest. In recounting these tales of adventure and discovery, I did not want to anthropomorphize the animals of Ravenwood, but my observations revealed many human characteristics in their behavior. I noticed that real animals demonstrate different personalities and appear to display emotions that reminded me of people I had met on my life's journey. Consequently, in these stories I conceded to ascribe some human emotions, tears, and a literary voice to the animals' responses to the situations they faced; sadness at the death of a friend, relief after a close escape, and joy at birth. The other descriptions of the animals' features and their behavior come from observation of them in their natural environment.

I learned from Topper other details about the animals of Ravenwood, such as the way animals see the world around them. Each animal is equipped with the type of vision required to meet its needs. Some are equipped with night vision; others see colors in a spectrum unnoticed by humans. As color vision in animals is mostly dichromatic, I used the color spectrum visible to humans to describe the surroundings retold in these stories.

In addition to differences in color perception, the placement of an animal's eyes determines its view of the world. As a deer, Sidekick views the world two-dimensionally, which contributes to her simple philosophy. For Sidekick, something either is or is not. There is no area of uncertainty or place for the hypothetical.

To Topper, Ravenwood is a place where the emerald magic never ends. May the influence of Topper's lessons, as retold in this book, be carried in the hearts, thoughts, and actions of its readers.

Ravenwood

Hope for Tomorrow

Lost and Found

From the grassy knoll in Ravenwood, I could see the gray, billowing clouds of smoke and jets of fire burning everything in their path on the adjacent ridge. The sky was black with birds winging their way to safety, and there was horror in the stampede of bears, cougars, bobcats, elk, deer, and thousands of smaller inhabitants fleeing the heat of destruction. I wondered what caused the fire that now threatened my home and the existence of all that I cherished.

I had not always lived here in the mountains of the gods, but it is here where I learned most of the values important in life.

My life in these woods had begun several years earlier in another fire. I was just a young cat traveling with Maggie, an older woman who lived alone most of the time since her grown son had a family of his own. We were constant companions, Maggie and I. I purred as I listened to her recall adventures from earlier days when she was left alone to raise her son. As she smoothed out my fur and slid her hand under my hindquarters, she would hold me close to her face and look at me through welling tears.

"You are a handsome cat," she would say, "and a joy to my soul."

We had left our home among cornfields of mice in the Midwest to travel a long, bumpy Northwest mountain road that kept me groaning for days. Most road trips didn't bother me, but on this particular occasion the backflips and somersaults in my head and stomach kept me miserable. After four days of dodging flashes of sunlight and shadow cast by the tall forest trees, we turned onto a narrow road frequented by logging trucks. As we traveled along the mountain switchback, my ears plugged up. I was about to voice a few complaining meows and head for safety in the back seat when I was bounced into the air and suddenly thrown forward to the passenger footwell. I heard the screeching of brakes and saw the contents of the front seat head toward me.

In great fear, I scrambled and clawed my way up her leg and chest toward the arms of Maggie, who was gripping the steering wheel with all her might. For a brief moment I was face-to-face with her, seeing the fear in her eyes too. Every inch of her being was at attention, and her repeated gasps frightened me further. I clung desperately to the threads of her sweater. Back and forth I was tossed across her chest with each rapid change of direction, until my grip was broken and I was sent hurtling out of her open window into a patch of sword fern.

The hard landing knocked the breath out of me. I awkwardly rose from my dazed state, shook off a cloud of fern spores, and saw the car burst into flames as it slammed against the hillside. Maggie was nowhere to be found. A few more feet to the left and I would have been greeted by a giant red cedar. So, in this disastrous situation, the ferns were the beginning of my good fortune in this new place. The smell of smoke in the air from the fire now reminded me of the smoke and column of fire that day when I was left alone in a cedar forest, on a mountaintop, in an unfamiliar part of the Northwest as a cold dark fell.

I was still alive, which my mother would have said was a reason for hope in the future. I searched all night for Maggie once the flames burned down, and found her charred remains at daybreak. Gone were her gentle spirit and the security of her love. Without Maggie, there would be no more tasty canned meals, and no more pats of appreciation. Suddenly I was very tired. But sleep was impossible. My mind revisited the horrendous event and I panted frantically. I had to stop thinking about the tragedy, so I thought about other memories. I thought about my mother and siblings.

Like so many cats in the Midwest, my mother had been a pregnant stray when she was taken to the animal shelter for adoption. After two days in the warmth of the shelter, my five siblings and I were born. I was unlike my striped brown siblings. My mother said I looked like my father, a Maine coon cat who lost a fight with a raccoon a few days before I was born. Seven cats in one cage meant a lot of getting stepped on. I made it a practice to wait until the other kittens were settled in their spots before I climbed my way to the top of the cat pile. For this reason, my mother named me Topper.

Living in a small cage with so many siblings required a keen sense of spatial awareness and patience. A cat had to be careful when bathing not to extend a leg into the personal space of another. There was little room for individual expression. There was time for playing, bathing, sleeping, and eating, in which everyone was required to participate on schedule. Those were happy times, but even those memories were making me sad now. While a cat can't live forever in an animal shelter, I wasn't ready to leave when Maggie arrived to adopt me.

My mother was very proud that I was selected, and comforted to know that I would have a chance for a good life, but I was not anxious to leave my already happy life. I pleaded with her not to let me go beyond the cage walls. A dull pain invaded my chest and a lump formed in my throat. I shook my head a few times so that my black tears could not be seen dripping down the white fur on my face. I had never been alone before. No matter how crowded the cage was, it was preferable to the vast unknown beyond its bars. I had been told that curiosity could kill a cat, so I was content to stay where life was familiar. Mother, sensing my great concern, began licking my ears and cleaning my fur, preparing me for departure. She reminded me that the fun times in my past provided hope for more fun in the future.

In this present dark night, as in the past, Mother's early lessons prepared me for future challenges. Because of the affection and confidence conveyed in her words, I knew I would be able to face whatever challenges lay ahead.

"I love you, Mom," I shouted toward the mountains and listened to each fading echo.

"Good-bye, son," came the memory of her whisper as I dozed off to sleep. "Stay on top."

In the morning light, the sound of disturbed air beneath the wings of a large black bird slowly circling overhead turned my attention from sweet dreams toward breakfast. As a domesticated feline, I had caught a few sparrows while Maggie wasn't watching, so I was reasonably confident in my ability to catch this bird too. As it neared me, its silhouette grew larger. I followed it as it passed over me to land on a cedar branch about twenty feet above the ground.

As silently as possible, I crept through the overgrowth of ferns at the base of the tree. I was considering a path up its trunk when the bird spread its wings and soared to a distant tree. Again I approached it, and again it repeated its maneuver, until finally it looked down and scolded me. "Gawk! Gawk! Gawk!" I was uncertain of what the bird was trying to communicate in its brash cry.

Looking about me, I realized that this bird had led me quite a distance into the woods. I could no longer see the road from the previous night. With nothing to lose, I jumped onto the trunk of the tree and started climbing, pausing now and then for rest as I spiraled up the trunk. Finally I was directly beneath the bird and realized it was larger than I had originally thought. Even if I managed to catch it, I would have more meat than I needed in one day. Looking down to see how far up I'd come, I noticed a deer staring up at me.

"What are you doing up there?" Her voice was slow and quiet.

"I'm hunting."

She snorted. "A little thing like you trying to catch a raven? Really? He's much too large for you. You must be new around here." She chomped a long stem of grass that slowly slipped into the side of her mouth. "What's your name?"

"Topper."

"Well, Topper, why don't you come on down before that raven decides you'd do fine for his breakfast?"

I looked down and thought descending was easier said than done. I carefully made my way down backward.

When I finally reached the bottom, I explained to my new friend what had happened the evening before.

"Well, that explains all of the forest activity this morning. Hearing the explosion last night, I wondered what today would bring. I suppose you know very little about life in the big woods. Am I right?"

"I don't even know where I am anymore," I stated. I looked down at my feet and then back up at her.

The doe shook her head, flapping her large ears.

"You're standing in Ravenwood, an ancient forest in the mountains of the gods," she responded.

I observed the area around me, filled with tall cedars, hemlocks, alders, and firs. The ground cover was thick with new shoots of sword and bracken ferns, and patches of stinging nettles. Beyond the clearing I could see the majestic peaks of rugged, snowcapped mountains. It was truly an area of great splendor.

What I had hoped would be my breakfast sat perched on a long overhead limb, chiding me in a loud voice.

"The raven you were hunting is the surveyor of this area. He and his family fly overhead twice a day, keeping the inhabitants of Ravenwood informed. He led you to safety within these woods. You should be grateful to him. Why do you want to eat him?"

"I'm hungry and there's no one to feed me. I'm not helpless. I've caught lots of birds, big birds and fast birds. I've never caught one quite this big, but I'm real hungry, so I'm sure I could," I said as I stood taller than before.

"Young one, you sure have a lot to learn about surviving out here. I'll take you down to the stream. You can catch yourself a fish while we start the lessons … that is, if you want to learn."

"Lessons? What lessons?"

The doe circled me, sniffed my head and tail, and then introduced herself as Sidekick. She said her beginning in these woods hadn't been so different from mine, and assured me that since she had survived, there was hope for me too.

I followed the doe to the stream before her dust could settle. My youthful agility enabled me to catch a salmon fry very quickly. I offered a morsel to my new friend.

"I appreciate the offer, Topper, but I'm a Columbian black-tailed deer. I prefer a diet of grass, grains, flowers, and twigs. But thank you for offering to share."

After breakfast I followed her through the woods, listening to the story of her early plight.

"I had lagged behind while my mother entered the middle of the road and waited for us twins to cross. As my brother obediently followed my mother, a truck with a full load of western cedars rounded the corner on a downhill grade and changed my life forever."

As a young orphan, her best bet had been to follow the deer herd, to learn from a distance as the does instructed their fawns. For this reason they called her Sidekick. As one who had always brought up the rear and eaten last, she was a study in patience and humility.

"I guess the first thing you should learn is to understand my signals," she stated. "You must pay close attention to my ears, tail, and eye folds, and to the position of my head." She flicked each one in turn. "Since my eyesight isn't as good as my hearing, my ears always turn first toward the direction of a sound."

She pulled off a leaf of salal, chewing it slowly as she explained how she never left her head down very long while she ate. She always kept her ears moving around to detect noise from all directions.

"When I'm startled, my tail stands up and I hold my head high, searching for the source of concern." Sidekick demonstrated and explained how her eyes were good for detecting motion, but not for detecting a camouflaged, stalking predator. Her eyes searched for changes in shapes and shadows.

It was important for me to notice everything in the world around me: sounds, shapes, patterns, and habits. "Observation is essential for survival," she warned. "When I flee, I spring with high leaps off all four legs, bounding over tree stumps and obstacles, spending more time in the air than on the ground to protect my legs. If I flee, don't follow me. Head in a different direction and go to our meeting place. A predator will have to decide which one of us to chase, and that second of indecision may provide both of us with the necessary time to escape. Do you understand?"

I nodded and agreed to help keep watch, since my eyesight was much better, especially at night. With her excellent senses of smell and hearing, we could survive much better working as a team.

As we approached an area with eight grazing deer, she explained deer habits. "Listen, deer have different personalities just like other animals. It's important that you understand the strengths and weaknesses of each one to avoid problems. The tall one on the right is called Queenie. She's the oldest doe in our herd, and everyone respects her wishes. When the bucks aren't around, she decides when and where we go.

"Next to her, with a scarred bump on her right hind leg and elongated hooves, is Matie, and alongside is her fawn, Tiny. They are very friendly and avoid confrontations with the other deer. They'll be good friends to you once they get to know you. Pretty Lady is between her two fawns. She has no physical flaws and is the favorite doe of Young Buck and Starbuck. They duel for her attention each November. Her young son, Tanner, may be Prince of Ravenwood someday. The last one is Madge, the mother of Midge. She often provokes fights if anyone grazes too closely.""

"Midge certainly is small," I commented.

"That's right," she agreed, "and Madge fights to protect the food supply, hoping that someday Midge will eat enough and gain stature."

As I watched, Madge raised one foot and brought it down sharply on the back of a fawn who had entered her grazing area.

"Ouch!" I exclaimed. "That must have hurt."

"Madge gives a quick kick as a warning blow. If the offender doesn't leave, she rises up on her back legs and fights with her front feet. Her hooves can easily cut through any hide, so heed her warnings."

"Aren't there any males around here?" I asked. I scratched diligently at my right ear, which had just been invaded by a fly.

"The bucks aren't here today," she replied, "but you should know their warnings too. A buck with antlers will lower his head and use a scooping motion as a warning. After that, a thrust of his antlers into a rib cage is very convincing.

"During the winter, when they have no antlers, they behave differently. You have to watch their ears and the skin fold at the inner corner of the eye. If the head goes up, the ears lie back, and the eye skin folds open wide, watch out. Deer always mean business when these inner skin folds of their eyes open wide."

I observed the characteristics of each grazing deer. "Is this your entire family?" I asked.

"Goodness, no!" she replied. "We number about twenty in all. There are other deer beyond the ridge, but they don't venture here very often. We generally travel in groups of eight to twelve. Once a week we meet up with the other group, and the twenty of us discuss the food supply. If you decide to hang around, you'll meet them in a few days."

As we headed toward the herd for introductions, Sidekick reminded me that to them, I resembled a civet cat in color and a bobcat in shape—two species undesirable to deer.

"When they hear us," she instructed, "sit still and let them approach you. Do not flip your tail or do anything that might suggest a threat. They will approach you cautiously, stretch their necks, sniff the air around you, and then bob their heads in an attempt to flush you. Just remain calm and let them know you pose no threat to them. Lower your head when Queenie passes, and if you must keep watch, keep your head down while you look up."

My introduction to Sidekick's herd went well. I followed her advice to the letter and was graciously accepted. It was good to have a family again, and I wanted to do my part to help protect the herd. At night I stayed close to Sidekick, watching the shadows for potential threats, but even so, I noticed that she always heard the noise before I located its source.

"What's that?" she said one time. "I heard something moving near that thicket. Do you see anything?"

I searched the darkness and initially saw nothing. After a few moments, she said she heard it again, so I strained harder to detect the slightest movement.

"I think I see something!" I whispered.

"Describe it," she insisted.

"It's bigger than I am; has black markings and rings on its legs."

"What's it doing?"

"I don't know. I can't see enough of it. The thicket is too dense." I saw her sniffing the air, expanding her nostrils.

"Do you smell anything?" I asked.

"No. It must not be a civet. They leave an odor when they rub against a rock or tree. Can you see the ears on the animal? What shape are the ears?" she asked more frantically.

"They look pointed like mine."

"Then it must be a bobcat." she surmised. "We'd better leave before it notices us. Stay on my path, Topper."

I followed as Sidekick slowly raised alternate front legs high above the grass line and paused before quietly placing each on the ground. Each hind foot filled the teardrop hoof print of its leader. I stayed low to the ground, just a stride behind her.

"Sidekick?" I asked, after we traveled a safe distance. "Why are you afraid of a bobcat? It's much smaller than you."

"They are very powerful for their size and are good climbers," she responded. "Often they prey on rabbits and rodents, but last year one killed a young deer in our herd by leaping on its back and biting its neck."

Her neck shivered as though to shake the memory loose.

"They stay within the territory they mark with feces and urine. We must have crossed into it. Usually an animal kills only when it's hungry or frightened, but there are also those who break all the rules for no obvious reason."

"Rules? What rules do you mean?" I inquired.

"Rules of Ravenwood. The things I've been trying to teach you the past few days. Rule number one: Notice everything. Remember? Observation of details is essential to survival."

I remembered the instruction, but I hadn't realized it was part of a set of rules.

"Rule number two: Do no harm. All animals must eat, but we must learn to eat wisely, taking only what we need to survive, so we don't disturb the delicate balance of nature. For example, if you had killed the raven the first day you were here, you would have killed more than you needed to survive. And, in doing so, you would have risked our lives by destroying our surveyor. Each creature has a purpose, and it is unwise not to respect its position in the food chain."

I was glad Sidekick had interrupted my hunt that first day, saving me from committing such a grave mistake.

"Rule number three: Own nothing. The animals in this forest belong to Ravenwood. It does not belong to them. We each roam freely while respecting the habits of others. Since we own nothing, we are not obligated through jealousy to protect any unequal distribution of land, trees, or stream."

I thought back to life in the animal shelter, and remembered how possessive we were as kittens of our few toys. Mother had to keep us from fighting all the time.

"During the winter, the heavy mountain snows force the cougars to follow the river, seeking food at lower elevations. We understand this and adjust our routines accordingly, avoiding the river area," Sidekick explained.

I had witnessed the excellent running and jumping ability of young cougars, and I had also heard some of the different sounds they made in an attempt to lure me into the woods.

"We don't risk our lives to protect the grasses," continued Sidekick. "Like the birds, many animals migrate to an area more conducive to winter survival and return in the spring to their homes, still unabused by those who shared it during winter."

We approached bushes covered with ripening berries, but Sidekick walked on by, only raising her nose to sniff their enticing fragrance.

"The black bears rest when it's cold, and wait for the berries to develop," Sidekick continued to explain. "We know that they eat many different things, such as insects, grasses, acorns, and animals. But berries are their delicacy, so we eat very few as we roam the woods. Taking an extra mouthful of berries is not worth the risk of encountering a six-feet-tall, 350-pound hungry bear.

"If we stay informed and act reasonably in the way we live our lives, we afford others an opportunity to do the same." Sidekick turned her head to look at me with her soft brown eyes.

We stopped walking to rest. I looked over at Sidekick, listening attentively as she elaborated on the three rules of the forest. I had not left her side for two days. She rested now on a cushion of branches beneath a cedar. As I kept a vigilant watch over my new friend, I reflected on these rules that I had not known existed. In my previous life as Maggie's cat, I was only concerned with eating, bathing, playing, and sleeping. The experiences of recent days made me aware that my other, self-indulgent, and supposedly independent life had changed. I realized that my existence and my actions had an impact on other animals and the forest around me.

The lessons I learned from Sidekick during my first two days prepared me well for the long summer ahead in Ravenwood. Summer days were pleasant with a slight breeze and low humidity. We roamed in sunlight for nearly sixteen hours each day. This was a welcome change from the Midwest, where I sheltered from daylight temperatures that scorched the earth, and where high humidity made breathing saturated air difficult.

By late summer I had followed Sidekick along every deer trail in the forest on our side of the ridge. I felt very confident in my ability to identify the animals and avoid confrontations as she had instructed.

Fishing filled my mornings, and hunting mice began at dusk. It was during one such hunt that I was distracted by the sound of breaking branches not far beyond the ridge. I climbed the trunk of an old hemlock and crawled out on its branch to look for the animal causing the disturbance. In a clearing below me were four brown bears, the likes of which Sidekick had never described. Each one was over eight feet in length and weighed about 1500 pounds. They were larger than any of the black bears that I had seen on our side of the ridge. I watched as they ate the vegetation in the clearing and played along the stream.

A scruffy-looking bear was digging in an anthill, licking its contents from his paw. The largest bear of the group paced between two trees, moving its two right legs together, then the two left in a swaying motion. After pausing to scratch its back on a tree, it yawned, and I realized it could easily carry a fawn in its mouth. As night fell, each bear went its separate way into the woods.

Before the morning sun had a chance to find me on the hemlock branch, I was awakened by a splashing sound in the river. A solitary brown bear was standing in the river, scooping out salmon and flipping them onto shore. On land it was a slow-moving bear, but in the river it was an adept fisher. The end of summer was nearing, and salmon were beginning to come upstream to spawn beyond the cascades.

A distant howling sound drew my attention downstream, where I noticed the treetops swaying in a wavelike motion, ushering a breeze toward the top of my tree. When it struck, I turned to make a quick descent but was too late. My support branch broke and I tumbled to the ground on the wrong side of the ridge. I fell with such force that I couldn't stop rolling down the hill toward the river—and toward the enormous bear.

My sudden and noisy arrival startled the bear, bringing it to its full height on two legs. With a loud roar and arms extended over its head, it had my undivided attention. I remained motionless, hoping it had not seen my location, but my anxious tail gave me away.

A representative of the largest bear species in the world approached within three feet of me, stopped, and then stood with front paws folded across its chest as it watched me cower. How I wished I had not been so curious the night before and fallen asleep on that branch. Sidekick would never know what happened to me because I had disobeyed her and wandered beyond our border. There would be no trace of me once this bear finished breakfast. If only I could find a way out of this situation, I'd never disobey an elder again. I kept my head low and stared up at the drooling bear.

"Gawk! Gawk! Gawk!" I heard from the treetop. It was Raven. The bear tossed his head and one paw non-threateningly toward the bird, then looked back at me. Did Raven want a piece of me too?

My tail wouldn't stop flipping. Slowly I placed one paw over its tip to hold it in place, not wanting to falsely pose a threat to such a large creature.

"Well, little fellow, you're a long way from home," commented the bear in a low, raspy voice. "Raven came to find you. He says there are deer beyond the hill who are pretty upset over your disappearance." There was a pause in his statement as his chuckle grew into a full laugh. "What do you have to say for yourself?"

I was beyond words. The bear was kind and enjoyed a good laugh. It wasn't aggressive or threatening. I pulled myself to my feet and shook the dust from my coat.

"I'm Topper, and I'm in a lot of trouble," I responded politely.

The bear, on all fours again, said with a nod, "Well, I'm Buddy, and I've certainly been in your tracks before. You'd better follow me back to the ridge and hightail it home."

I followed in his paw prints—his very large paw prints, paw prints so large that I could drink a day's worth of water from one puddle. Sidekick would never believe my adventure if she forgave me long enough to listen to it. Had she been the one to send Raven to my rescue?

"I'm sorry to have disturbed your fishing," I blurted out awkwardly. "I'm an avid fisher myself."

"Is that a fact? Well, what's your preference, king or coho?"

"Oh, I'm not too particular, as they all taste good to me. What's your favorite?"

"King salmon's the best for the effort," he said as he looked back over his shoulder toward the river, "but this year I've had to settle for coho, what with the streams running so low. Adaptation's my middle name, you know. What about you? Do you have a middle name?"

"No," I said apologetically. "I'm just Topper."

Buddy nudged me up the hill with his powerful nose and said, "That's a fine name, little fellow. It serves you well. I won't forget it."

"I won't forget you either," I shouted back as I crested the hill and turned toward home. "Good fishing to you, Buddy!"

"And to you!" replied his echo.

After several reminders about how foolish I had been, Sidekick found the compassion to forgive me. I told her about the brown bears and she informed me they were Kodiak bears, not native to this area. They had been brought here many years ago by humans, who trained them at a young age and then abandoned them as young adults. They normally stayed farther beyond the ridge, foraging for plant food, insects, and honey. Once a year they changed their diet from being primarily vegetarian to being carnivorous, feeding entirely on fish during the spawning season. I hoped that I would meet them again.

Hunters in the Forest

More than a month had passed since my encounter with Buddy, and I remained close to the herd. It was nearing the rut season, and more bucks joined us. Young Buck, a three-year-old with a kind heart, was my favorite. He had asymmetrical antlers and skinny hindquarters and was not particularly tall. His jousting partner was a handsome four-year-old named Starbuck, with broad shoulders, a wide forehead, and three paired points. I enjoyed watching them practice their techniques as I took my bath in a sun spot.

Young Buck wasn't very strong, but he was smart. He stood below Starbuck on the hillside, locked antlers with him, then wrestled until Starbuck pushed beyond his point of balance and stumbled down the hill. I was told they had wrestled for the attention of Pretty Lady in previous years, but this year I had my bets on Sidekick. She pretended not to notice them as she searched the ground for a few remaining wildflowers, but her eyes never left those of Young Buck. They had been friends since they were fawns, when Young Buck had protected her from the hooves of Madge on many occasions.

Since we had arrived early for our weekly grassy knoll meeting, I hid under a clump of long grass, watching for our cousin herd to arrive. They looked like our herd of twelve, but their names were native, labeling them according to how they lived their lives. Ka-newk was the leader, and the most feared. She was tall, with a face darker than the others, a long, high curve on her nose, and eyes that did not invite trust. The avaricious movement of her lips formed an awkward grimace, cunning and unnatural. She was closely accompanied by other does who were, according to Sidekick, not yet disgruntled with her tactics. Other cousins followed her herd, a potential warring faction, but kept their distance from her.

Her pawn today was Ha-nasus, a doe eager to please and very popular with the rest of the herd. Her job was to keep the disgruntled does in line, offering them solace in their defeats against Ka-newk.

Ba-Soht was on Ka-newk's right flank, where she had been all summer. Her gait was confident, but her eyes told a different story. Most animals are honest with themselves when they are thinking, but I couldn't detect anything truthful in her expression. A sinister-looking scar lined the right side of her face. Sidekick said Ba-Soht's face had once been so perfect that its beauty was admired by others. Now, the scar was a reminder of her confrontation with Ka-newk.

Ha-vas, a recent rejection from Ka-newk's court, noisily stumbled over twigs as she made her way on a separate path through the forest. She was obviously upset because deer are usually agile and silent creatures. Ke-naw followed her, offering words of encouragement.

"Where are the others?" Queenie asked as the meeting on the knoll began.

"Why ask me? I'm not their keeper," replied Ka-newk indifferently. "They're free to do as they wish. It's not my responsibility to worry about them."

I could see the anger churning in Queenie's eyes as she replied. "We're all free, but with freedom and leadership come responsibility. It is in the best interest of each one of us to care about others. We must maintain balance or we are all doomed. Have you learned nothing from your own experiences, Ka-newk?"

Ka-newk did not like to be challenged and never admitted guilt. She littered her life with cast-off friends, and resolved nothing in the process; yet, strangely, deer waited in line to become her favored friend.

Sidekick had befriended Ka-newk in their first year in Ravenwood at a time when the other deer chased Ka-newk from the grazing areas. Ka-newk accepted the friendship until she grew strong enough to dominate the others. Matie told me that Sidekick refused to be dominated, unlike the rogue group that followed Ka-newk when Queenie issued the ultimatum that destined them to live on the other side of the hill. Because it was a subject that Sidekick preferred not to discuss, I observed the situation from a distance to understand it for myself.

"My experiences," snarled Ka-newk, "have taught me to fend for myself and trust no one. Following a deer like you, Queenie, would mean missed opportunities for me."

"Then your expulsion from the herd was a blessing for us all," responded Pretty Lady in Queenie's defense.

Ba-soht said nothing, but stood close to Ka-newk, waiting for a command. Ka-newk's retort came with great anger. "Queenie imprisons you with her code of the forest, always insisting that you act in accordance with her will, plaguing you with guilt if you falter. There's no freedom in guilt. I give my deer complete freedom to do what they want."

"As long as they follow you without dissent," said Matie.

Ka-newk glared at Matie, her eye folds widening for a challenge.

"They follow me because they are free and admire my way of life," she retorted.

"No," said Sidekick calmly. "They follow you because they think they don't deserve anything better. Real freedom requires choice and respect. You teach apathy and submission. You have no respect for anything unlike yourself."

Sidekick's statement brought an abrupt end to the discussion. Even Ka-newk, in all her anger, could not veil the truth.

We waited all day, but the other three deer never arrived. Raven was asked to look, but returned without locating them. As Sidekick was still worried about her missing cousins the following morning, I offered to climb the tree on the ridge to look for them, adding that I thought they were probably all right. Her head hung low as we walked back home.

"You don't understand," she moaned. "It's near the end of fall now, and humans may be in the forest."

I did not understand Sidekick's concern about humans being nearby, since my only experience with them had been as my caregivers. I remembered them being predictable and saw no reason to fear their presence.

"Tell me about your humans," Sidekick asked hesitantly as we searched the woods again the following morning. "You've spoken kindly of Maggie, but have you known many others?"

"I liked her grandson," I replied eagerly. "He was a real charmer and quite active by cat standards. His pocket collection of string, pebbles, and other trinkets kept us entertained for hours as we rode through covered bridges spanning the cascading rivers to our favorite fishing holes. Oh, Sidekick, how I loved fish day! Once a week the community had a fish fry, and the humans gave me scraps to eat."

As Sidekick did not yet seem relieved, I continued.

"And I liked the shelter workers, who cleaned the cat cages, and the mailman who tossed me a daily morsel as he came through the front gate, and the elderly people we visited who had warm laps and tears in their eyes. Humans can be very kind, Sidekick. You don't need to worry about your cousins."

We approached a western red cedar that provided a nice lookout for me thirty feet above the ground. I was showered with a sprinkling of water as a gentle breeze stirred the rain-soaked foliage of the flexible branches above me. I could see the clearing and the forest beyond it, but there was no sign of the three cousins. At the edge of the forest, I watched as a spotted bobcat cleaned its short tail, a sign that breakfast was over. Its short hind legs and slightly tufted ears resembled mine, but she was much larger. Romping and rolling in the ferns nearby were her two kits.

The salmon were still active. Through the clear water of the mountain stream, I could see the bold, mature colors of the streamlined coho and the bronze, arched back of the much larger and bulkier chinook. I spent hours during the day sitting on a river rock, watching them circle at the base of the cascades before attempting an ascent. Every few minutes, one twisted through the air, hoping to reach the pool on the first level of rocks, where it could rest before its next ascent. More often than not, the body of the salmon fell short of the pool and slammed into the face of the boulder. Stunned briefly, it would slide back downstream to try again.

Impressed by their perseverance, I wondered if they knew what fate awaited them once they reached their destination and spawned. Sidekick said they were born in this stream and, after a year, followed it to the sea, where they spent several years of their lives before returning home. The life of these anadromous fish was difficult and I respected it; I was careful to eat only enough to keep me healthy and trim.

My attention was drawn to the trees again when I realized a great silence had fallen on the woods. There were no birds to be seen or heard, and the bobcat family had disappeared. I waited for something to stir, but nothing did. I could smell dust in the air. There was no sign of what had disturbed it.

To my right, near the border of the grassy knoll, I saw a glint of light traveling through the woods. I climbed to the other side of the tree to get a better look and saw a large pickup truck, similar to the one at the animal shelter. It was traveling toward the ridge, and the sunlight was glancing off one of its mirrors as it made its way along the switchback. Something very large was in the back of the truck, but it was still too far away for me to determine the contents.

I looked down at Sidekick. She had heard the noise. Her head was high, and her ears were pointed in the direction of the truck beyond the hill.

"It's okay," I reported. "The truck is stopping."

I watched as three men exited the truck and walked toward the stream. One pointed and shouted while the other two collected rocks and threw them in the salmon pool. The waters were muddied by the time they finished, and I could no longer see the salmon. From the backseat of the truck, they removed a cooler and drank from cans as they lounged on the ground. As I was getting tired, and my hindquarters were cramping from sitting so long on a narrow branch, I rose to begin my stretching routine.

Bang, bang, bang—bang, bang! echoed a piercing sound. I nearly fell from fright. Sidekick bounded in all directions as she screamed, "The hunters have guns, Topper! Hide, Topper, hide! They'll kill you!" She headed deep into the forest.

I had never heard Sidekick talk so quickly or anxiously. I decided I was as safe as I could be as long as the men didn't look for birds. The shooting continued until they had shot holes in every empty drink can. Theirs was the only sound in the forest, and that was too much. They made more noise than coyotes under a harvest moon.

All night the hunters paraded around the fire, shouting and prancing as they shot at shadows. The air was filled with human scent and buckshot. The raccoons, civets, and bobcats would not visit the river tonight.

Daylight dimmed under gray clouds as the humans loaded the cooler into the truck, leaving the cans, foil wrappers, and shell casings behind. As the truck circled the clearing on its departure, I could see the detailed outline of its rear cargo, now only partially covered by a tarp, and understood why it had been unrecognizable before.

The hair on my back stood erect in horror. A huge, burning lump formed in my throat, making swallowing difficult, and I panted. With weakened legs, I hugged the tree branch and shook black tears from my eyes. I was wrong. Sidekick had been wise to worry about humans. These creatures were not like Maggie or any other human I had encountered.

Sickened by human perversity, I mourned the sight of twelve thin legs extending over the side of the truck bed. Heaped in the bed lay the three gutted carcasses of Sidekick's cousins. Why had the hunters shown such disrespect for three graceful lives? With so much meat on one deer, why had they killed three? Animals wouldn't treat their prey with such ingratitude and waste. Animals celebrate a prey's quality of life and appreciate its position in the food chain. These humans seemed to celebrate only themselves and respect nothing.

Air that normally invigorated me now choked my breath. I descended the tree and followed the deer trail back into the woods. I found Sidekick with the rest of our herd and related the sad news. Queenie was furious with Ka-newk for not keeping watch over her group.

"You have endangered us all with your self-centeredness," she chided. "It's bad enough that our cousins were killed, but with such good hunting, the humans will tell others and more will return. We now live in constant danger from a voracious killer that has no respect for our laws, lives, or for Ravenwood … and you are to blame."

Queenie rose up on her hind legs and brought her front hooves down hard on the back of Ka-newk, chasing her through the forest. When Queenie returned, she ordered us not to roam during the day until the first snowfall. We were to travel in small groups at night, finding a different place to rest each day.

We moved on. Winter was not far away. I could feel my coat thickening because bath time required more work, pulling out the old fur and keeping the new in place. I later realized my fur was preparing for winter. The deer were also changing. Their winter coats were dark and slick, well suited to repel the winter rains. In the steady, cool temperatures, the weekly rains left puddles and moisture everywhere.

My fur required more frequent grooming, giving me less time to sleep.

Restriction to night activity meant encountering different animals: owls, bats, large cats, and the like. My main complaint was with the omnivorous raccoon. Frequently, my early morning fishing expeditions were interrupted by a foraging raccoon who brought his catch to the stream to moisten the food before eating. His stirring the waters frightened away any potential catch for my breakfast, which left me hungry and even more impatient.

"Why does he always bring his food to the river?" I complained. "Can't he eat first and drink later?"

"Well," said Sidekick thoughtfully, "perhaps he has no salivary glands to moisten his food and make swallowing easier."

Sidekick regarded my flustered state, adding, "Maybe the raccoon likes your company, but is afraid to say anything."

I laughed and admitted that the raccoon did have one physical characteristic that I envied. Like a squirrel, he could rotate his hind feet, thus giving him the ability to descend a tree either headfirst or tail first. I could climb quickly, but my descent was slowed because I had to exit in reverse until I was close enough to the ground to safely jump.

One winter's day, after the sky had dropped a foot of snow overnight, Queenie informed us that other animals had not seen humans in our area for some days, so we could once again roam freely during the daylight. With this much snow, grass was in short supply, so the deer covered more miles each day in search of food. As ice on the river prevented me from enjoying my typical breakfast entree, I had to spend more time searching for small rodents.

While absorbing the warmth of a sunny spot on an exposed rock, I noticed a rabbit scurrying in a serpentine pattern in a nearby clearing. I walked closer to explore a mound of dirt. The snow had melted in this sunny location, and I could see a rather large hole on the side of the mound that exposed a very inviting tunnel. Slowly I crept closer, looking from side to side.

I approached the entrance, heard a sharp bark, and saw the head of a large rodent pop out of the cavity. It displayed its molars while a second one crawled out to protest my invasion of its territory. I circled the mound, examining their grayish coats, and contemplated whether I should prey upon such a large rat.

Sidekick had heard their yipping and came to instruct me.

"You do realize that you've stirred up a coterie of prairie dogs and not rats, don't you?"

I was embarrassed. I had not seen prairie dogs before. Their heads and teeth were the same shape as other rodents', but their bodies were much larger and their tails were tipped in black. As I was more curious than hungry, I apologized for the intrusion and slipped away. "Sidekick, this is not a prairie. What are they doing here?" I asked.

"Humans brought them here as gifts to a child. After a few months, the humans lost interest in them and used them as live bait in a trap on the ridge. Buddy heard their whimpering, sprung the trap, and turned them loose."

"How awful!" I exclaimed.

"Yes, but everything worked out all right," reported Sidekick. "Buddy taught them to adapt. Since they are strictly vegetarians, they dug their home in the clearing where grass was prevalent. They're a nice family. Right now they're rather busy with pups, whose eyes haven't opened yet. They're spending all of their time underground. It's better if we visit them in the summer."

To my amazement, Sidekick seemed to know everything and everyone. I wanted to be as smart when I got to be her age. On our way back to the herd, she introduced me to the Roosevelt elk that spent the winters in the protected mountain valleys of Ravenwood. They were giants compared to the deer. She explained that the yodeling whistle sound we had heard in the fall was a male elk bugling, and this summer we might see the new calves before the herds moved to higher elevations.

There was so much to learn about life in Ravenwood. I looked at Sidekick's unimposing stature, leisurely gait, tender brown eyes, and fur as soft as pollen. Her quiet example in the remote ranks of the herd defined leadership, encouraging me to follow.

Misplaced Pride

When spring arrived, the mountain meadows were painted in white, red, yellow, and orange wildflowers. Ravenwood was the perfect place for endless exploration. The arenas for my schooling were now foggy lowlands, lush meadows, and forests so thick in alder, hemlock, fir, and cedar that snow reached the ground only after melting from the branches. Bigleaf maples were beginning to bud, and wildlife which had been dormant during the winter now greeted the glorious bright days.

One aromatic day, Sidekick took me to the highest point in Ravenwood. From there, I could see beyond our forest. The moist ground beneath our feet was covered in lichen and fern. Moss-carpeted logs provided me a bridge over sorrel and salal, keeping my coat dry. Oregon grape lined the deer trails. Rows of stilt-like roots grew around nursery logs, using every inch of available space for plant life. The branches of fallen cedars were reaching for the sky, creating a row of new trees where only one had stood before.

The area we were approaching was home to Sitka spruce, Douglas fir, and three-hundred-feet-tall western hemlocks. Mountains rose from the ocean shore, trapping the moist air, cooling it, and causing the resulting clouds to dump large quantities of rain on their west side. Much less fell, however, in their rain shadow. Alpine glaciers carved into the slopes of mountain peaks above the tree line. Ravenwood existed in a diverse and isolated green world, surrounded on three sides by salt water. Through the seasons I was learning about the powerful force that created this paradise. From Sidekick, I learned this awesome, creative force was to be respected.

"Ravenwood is such a wonderful place, I shall never leave," I commented to Sidekick as we arrived at the viewpoint.

"Ravenwood is not so much a location as it is a state of mind; a quality of thought and energy; a way of life," she replied thoughtfully. Pointing to the eagle soaring overhead, Sidekick explained how the eagle could use what it learned from the treetops of Ravenwood no matter where it went.

"Not all that grow up here, stay here," she reminded me. "There's a little bit of Ravenwood everywhere. If you leave, the rules of Ravenwood go with you."

I quietly recited to myself the three rules while surveying the land of Ravenwood, where beauty was in search of emotion. "Number one: Notice everything. Number two: Do no harm. Number three: Own nothing. See, I still remember them," I said out loud, with an ounce of pride attached. Expecting new rules to follow, I asked, "What's next?"

"Three rules are enough if you remember to live them," stated Sidekick. My pride sank back toward my knees.

I raised my nose toward the breeze, breathing deeply the scent of the rainforest around me; its fragrance was not to be forgotten.

The route home took us along our north ridge border, where whitecaps on the ocean tide could be seen rolling toward shore. Flocks of gulls cruised the shallow waters, loons dove for supper, and cormorants rested on floating logs, drying their outstretched wings.

"It's time to head back," Sidekick said, cropping a patch of grass.

I was reluctant to leave, but I knew she was right. Shaking a few pesky flies off her back, she tossed her head toward the sky, as though to wave the moon awake and headed back to the familiar grove of cedars with me close behind, flicking at flies with my tail.

Now, a cat's tail is a source of pride, and there was certainly no reason for me to be ashamed. Mine was a fluffy, full plume of black-and-white fur that I held high as I paraded through the forest. So spectacular was this distinguished flag that it required much attention to keep it free of burrs. A deer flags its tail when it is startled or excited, but I flagged mine at every opportunity. There were times when I would not have been seen at all walking through the sword ferns had it not been for the top of my tail dancing above the fronds. The admiration that I held for my tail was the cause for a lesson on misplaced pride.

Ka-newk had a mountain-size ego that she used to fashion her court. Surrounded by those who offered no challenge to her ideas or self-appointed status, she was seldom alone. I never discovered the reason for her ego, but I learned of its effects.

Sidekick had taught me to cherish life, no matter how devoid of value it seemed. In theory, this seemed easy. We identified the importance of every creature, from slugs to cougars, that lived in the woods. But in the presence of Ka-newk, the ideal seemed unobtainable. She was late to every knoll meeting, making a grand entrance as she paraded past the rest of us who respected the nonrenewable resource of time. Her erect stance did not invite friendly conversation, and with eyes that intermittently beckoned and dismissed, one never knew what scheme to expect from her. For several months, I observed her calculated manipulations, and I wanted no part of her world. As she refused to consider helpful recommendations from Queenie and Sidekick, there was no hope for future change in her antics. Besides, I saw no room for her on the animal chart between the slugs and cougars!

Even though the herd had survived the threat of human hunters, there was still a sense of urgency in Queenie as she nervously pawed the ground. She reminded us that although the hunters were gone, some of their traps might still be in the forest. While a trap was not large enough to kill a deer, stepping in one could sever a leg and make an injured animal easy prey for cougar or bobcat. I heeded her caution, carefully examining the trails for signs of traps and other hazards as the herd moved through the woods.

The winter snow had been wet. Its weight in the treetops caused cedars to bend and firs to break. In addition, the forest floor was a maze of fallen alders, whose shallow roots in moist ground could not support the leaning trees. In some instances, these new obstacles changed our course, requiring more bounding through the woods.

A tall stump provided me a vantage point from which to view the trails as I shook a dusting of snow from my tail.

"Hey, tomcat, why waste time grooming yourself? You're so low on the food chain that nobody gives you a second thought. Only a lowlife like Sidekick would give you a minute of her day."

I didn't have to look up; I knew it was Ba-soht taunting me. Just like always. She certainly spent a lot of time reminding me how I wasn't worth her time.

"You hear me, tomcat? Why don't you just leave these woods? You're not one of us. If Queenie had any sense, she'd run you out. I know Ka-newk wouldn't waste a minute getting rid of you."

I rolled over and continued bathing without raising my head. Discouraged that she hadn't riled me, Ba-soht returned to the side of Ka-newk. The two of them continued their jeers. Stretching seemed to be a nice distraction from their insults, so I stretched every part of me that could be stretched, and some parts twice. As their insults continued, I tried to walk away from them along a crumbling old-growth log suspended a few feet above ground. Ka-newk pursued me. Using her long legs to jump over me, she crossed the log, landing about six feet to my left. I ducked and lost my footing on the log.

Looking toward the ground, I regained my balance and noticed the faint outline of a trap, lightly covered with leaves and branches, about three feet ahead of me on the left side of the log. Ka-newk did not see it. She had forgotten the first rule of the forest and did not notice the slight change in her environment. Her devilish eyes were on me, not on the ground.

Ba-soht was still to my right, using every word in her limited vocabulary to insult me. I sat still, listening to their words drive daggers into my heart. A branch snapped. I saw Ka-newk step toward me.

"No!" I shouted. "Stay away!"

Her left foot was only inches from the steel trap now. I didn't want her to get hurt, and I warned her again to stay away. But she wouldn't stop. I knew Queenie would be upset if another deer got injured, and I respected Queenie too much to disappoint her.

"Stay away!" I shouted again. "You'll get hurt."

"Scared, are you?" she snarled. "Nobody around to protect you, you little ball of fluff? Do you really think that something as small as you could hurt me? Say good-bye, you worthless hairball!"

Then a shadow passed over me. I looked up to see Ba-soht leaping over the log in front of me, her shorter legs just clearing its mossy carpet. There was no time to warn her, and nothing she could do would change her situation in midair. She was headed straight for the trap. I gritted my teeth and jumped down hard on the branch lying across the trap. Its iron jaws snapped shut, just missing my hindquarters, but catching my tail two inches lower.

I fell to the ground. The pain was intolerable. I felt nauseated and started to faint. The iron jaws had cut clear through my tail, leaving me with a short stub that was bleeding and throbbing profusely. Oh, the agony, the throbbing, the blanket of cold fear was too much!

Sidekick and Matie heard my cry and ran over to help. Matie nuzzled and licked me while Sidekick dug with the points of her hooves and mashed mud on my stub. The world seemed to be rolling sideways; the air seemed too thick for me to breathe. My eyes closed effortlessly. I heard the distant voices of Ka-newk and Ba-soht telling the others how I had gotten what I deserved for leading them into danger.

When I opened my eyes, I saw the distinct elongated hooves of Matie next to me. I had lost my plume of pride, but my stump was beginning to feel less painful. The mud pack had stopped the bleeding, and most of the swelling disappeared after a few stub soakings in the cold mountain stream.

"Don't keep it in the water too long," Sidekick warned. "You don't want it to become fish bait."

She was trying to make me laugh, but I didn't feel much like laughing. I missed my tail and had nothing to show for its sacrifice. The cousins still taunted me and didn't even acknowledge my sacrifice. I had not told Sidekick what really happened, and she had not asked.

"Feeling pretty low, are you?" she said with a mouth full of grass.

"Yeah. I just want to sit and think." I moaned.

"It's better not to," she countered. "Animals are judged more by how they respond in an instant than by what they plan in a lifetime."

I looked up and saw her wink at Matie and Tiny.

"Raven told us all about what really happened," said Tiny.

"Some animals spend a lot of time thinking about what to do, and then make the wrong choice," continued Sidekick. "You didn't think at all and made the right choice."

"There's nothing noble about the animosity I feel toward Ka-newk and Ba-soht."

Sidekick gave me a hard nudge that sent me tumbling down the hill.

"Your feelings of anger are perfectly normal under the circumstance," Sidekick consoled me. "You aren't expected to like everyone you meet. What's noble is your decision to keep the laws of Ravenwood alive, despite your feelings." She followed me down the hill and found a grove of cedars for a shady rest.

"The second rule states "do no harm." If you had not acted as you did, Ba-soht would have been injured, the herd would have been harmed, and the rule would have died a little for lack of use. But Topper, while your action was important to the herd, you must also think of your own safety, for injury to you also affects the herd."

"But Ka-newk and her followers don't even believe in the rules, so what good did it do?" I pleaded.

"The rules don't only protect those that believe in them. They exist to benefit all creatures. Obedience to the rules helps maintain nature's critical balance. It isn't enough to obey only some of the rules; we must obey all rules to preserve the delicate balance in our lives."

"Sidekick, you know I want to do my part. I want to help preserve this way of life in Ravenwood, but some of what you say is really hard for me to understand."

"That's understandable, Topper. You've had a difficult few days. I just want you to know that I'm proud to be your friend. Some animals spend a lifetime trying and never achieve such understanding, even in adulthood. But you've managed to achieve it in your youth," Sidekick said.

Feeling a little better, I bounded down to the river the following morning, jumped onto the slippery rock of my fishing perch, and immediately slid into the water. It caused such a disturbance that salmon was no longer an item on the breakfast menu. Without my long tail, I had no counterbalance that had previously prevented such embarrassments. Cats learn quickly the importance of center of gravity in maintaining balance, and I was flustered to have forgotten its role at my age.

Raccoon was moistening his final meal before resting for the day, and chided me for giving him an unexpected bath. The rocky tumble irritated my injured tail, causing my hindquarters to throb as I limped back into the woods.

For two days I was stiff and sore. Sidekick worried about me not eating, but I simply couldn't move, and not moving or eating only made me weaker. There was nothing my deer family could do. They did not have the necessary skills to catch fish, birds, or rodents, and I didn't care much for grass or fruit.

Early on the morning of the fourth day, I awoke to the smell of fresh salmon. Lying beside me in a small puddle was a young pink salmon. I looked around, but saw no one to thank for this gift. I ate it slowly, enjoying every bite. As I sat up to begin the after-meal bath ritual, I noticed tiny footprints with no heel marks leading from the water to me, and then back into the trees.

The next morning the same thing happened, only this time my breakfast was a bird. Again, there was no one to thank. I decided to wake early the next day to watch for my provider. Sure enough, just before dawn, I saw a shadowy figure, long tail in the air, approach me with two mouse tails dangling from its mouth.

"So it's you, Raccoon, that I have to thank for my meals."

He placed the entree beside me.

"Ah, it's no trouble. I'm glad to do it. I wouldn't want to lose my tail either, but I'm sure you'll learn to get along. Sorry I yelled at you the other day for getting me wet. It's just that, well, I hadn't planned on a morning bath."

I had been slow to trust Raccoon since my father had been killed by one. Perhaps living by the rules of Ravenwood makes a difference in animals. I wondered if Raccoon's actions were part of the balance Sidekick had mentioned. As he headed back to his family, I shouted after him, "You're all right, you know."

"Not bad yourself," he said, chuckling over his shoulder.

By the end of the week, I was getting around much better and was ready to attend the meeting at the grassy knoll. Summer was creeping from the lowlands toward the mountains, but it was still spring in Ravenwood. In the cool dampness, the deer were cleaning their fur, removing any dirt that might allow moisture to penetrate their coats and chill the skin. The snow had melted, leaving behind a sedimentary rock garden soon to be ablaze with new growth. The skies were clear, and the faint outline of Lilliputian trees that separated the alpine and subalpine areas of the ridge above us denoted their vigorous struggles. To the left was the barren path of an avalanche: evidence of the violence that threatens all forms of life in the mountains during the wintery months. Soon, flowers and berries would punctuate the bushes, encouraging us all to forget the harsh winter.

I had expected Ka-newk to resume her usual taunting of me, but she was unusually friendly toward everyone. Perhaps it was the promise of summer in the air that had changed her demeanor, but I was still wary of the wintery side of her nature. Working her way through the herd, she complimented each deer. Her sly manner succeeded in making the others feel important and privileged to be her friend, and they confided in her more information than she should know.

In their giddiness, they spoke of nothing else until the end of the day when Ka-newk announced her intention to challenge Queenie as leader of the herd. Queenie was too old to travel far, and Ka-newk, next in succession, could lead the herd forward to better grazing areas—or so she said. We were to consider the challenge for a week and vote at the following meeting. Everyone understood the importance of this vote. It would determine the future direction and personality of the herd. A leader had the responsibility of teaching the wisdom of the herd to successive generations, working to secure the future today.

All week long, the deer stressed over the decision until the time to vote arrived.

A hush fell on the knoll as each herd member circled to cast a vote. As expected, Ba-Soht and Ha-nasus cast their support for Ka-newk. I glanced at the others who flanked Ka-newk, hoping they would finally act in accordance with their thoughtful, analytical natures instead of from fear.

Sidekick looked at Ka-newk, determined to bring to the forefront the sensitive issues at stake.

"Which way is forward?" she asked, in her straightforward manner.

Everyone seemed surprised by the question, especially Ka-newk.

"What do you mean?" sputtered Ka-newk. "That's a ridiculous question! Stop provoking an argument. Just cast your vote."

"I can't vote," replied Sidekick, "until I know the answer. You claim you are next in succession and you will lead us forward. All I want to know is, in your mind, which way is forward?"

With great agitation, Ka-newk pointed her nose toward the hills and said, "Through the forest toward the mountains is forward, of course. Now, what is your vote?"

Sidekick looked carefully at the area between the river and the mountains and replied, "I'll have to cast my vote for Queenie, because you are wrong. Your direction is backward."

Ka-newk and her followers reared on their hind legs and stomped around in a fury, sliding in the mud, leaving divots where tender grass was stripped away. Loud snorts of the outraged deer echoed through the woods, stirring to attention Raven and resting passerines.

"How dare you make such an outrageous claim! What proof do you have that forward is toward the river?" they bellowed.

In her authoritative manner, Queenie stepped to the center of the circle and asked us to follow her to the river, where each herd member could examine the situation from the same point of view. Once we arrived at the river's edge, we stood with our backs to the river and looked toward the mountains. Sidekick was right! From our new position, the forest succession was obvious. At our feet, on the river's edge, was bare ground, a perfect surface for the new seedlings of a future forest. A few feet away, beyond the young saplings, could be seen the light green leaves of the bigleaf maples. Farther toward the mountains were the fast-growing firs, followed by the more shade-tolerant hemlocks. The deeper we looked into the forest, the more old-growth cedars we saw. Some of the trees in the deep forest were as ancient as their soil and were now in their final stage of development. To walk toward the mountains and away from the river was to move backward in time, from young growth along the river to old growth near the mountains. Where we stood at the river's edge was the beginning of the future.

Sidekick was right, but the rest of us had required a metaphor to understand it. It took a river for us to discover our future. I looked back at Sidekick, but I could barely see her. The sunlight was not shining on her as much as it appeared to be shining through her, illuminating the river rapids beyond.

Ka-newk lost her challenge that day without ever understanding the hardship her poor reasoning could have inflicted on the herd. Fortunately, the majority of the herd understood that staying with Queenie afforded us possibilities for the future. Following Ka-newk meant a journey through the past, and her past wasn't a place most of us wanted to experience more than once.

As we walked along the river valley on our return home, the landscape opened into grasslands. There I saw elk and their calves before they headed back into the cool, high country for summer. The spotted newborns struggled to their feet from a curled position close to their mothers. In a few weeks they would be agile: jumping streams, dodging predators, and climbing steep trails. Watching them reminded me of the lesson that Sidekick said was to be learned from their rut combat.

Each fall, the mature males rubbed the summer velvet from their antlers to sharpen their tines. After bugling their intentions, the contenders would approach each other while the prized cows observed from the hillside. Some challengers were uncertain and retreated. Others wasted no time in attacking. Around and around they circled, looking for the opportune moment, lunging forward, locking antlers, snorting. They kicked up dirt, twisting and turning, battling until death or fatigue overcame them. So stubborn were some bulls that they continued the fight until both died of exhaustion. The more cunning bulls avoided battle altogether and used the distraction that the fights of others created as an opportunity to entice the cows.

In any case, Sidekick said the lesson to be learned from the elk was that the prize for which one fights isn't always awarded to the mighty victor. Sometimes it is taken by those who choose not to fight, and sometimes there are no victors.

I appreciated the timeliness of Sidekick's lessons that prepared my thoughts before my own challenges arrived. In this emerald world, forces of creation and decay, life and death, existed simultaneously, as evidenced in the carcass of a decaying log that provided a nursery for infant trees. A choice between life and death was not always available, and so it was important to respect both.

"Topper," Sidekick explained patiently, "it is important for you to understand that the seasonal deluge of rain in these broad valleys and vast coniferous mountain forests provides the only home in the world for some plant and animal species. That is the reason the rules of Ravenwood are vitally important. With so many plants and animals dependent on this ecosystem, our deer herd relies on wise leadership that constantly observes the animal at the top of the food chain to determine the health of our environment. If the cougar and eagle, which feast on smaller animals, continue to thrive, then we know our streams and plant life are healthy."

"I understand, Sidekick," I remarked, hoping to assure her. "Disregarding the rules by consuming too much is done at our own peril. Taking more than we need not only deprives another of food, but if what we consume is toxic, we doom ourselves by overeating."

"Exactly, Topper. As our host, Ravenwood survives through a sacred, symbiotic trust with all its guests. Any harm to this environment could mean the end of an entire species."

"Just as making the wrong decision through misplaced pride can lead to weakening of the herd and possibly to its demise," I added.

Our deer herd paused to look around us, taking in the majesty of the mountainous backdrop and the luminous shades of green.

"Look at the detail," said Sidekick, tilting her head toward the sky and treetops.

Above us, low clouds gathered below the serrated peaks, hugging the steep slopes, bringing the promise of more rain later in the day. The tree branches looked blurred, draped in club moss that found its nourishment from sunlight, air particles, and moisture. Overhead, glimpsed through spaces between tree branches, a pair of bald eagles soared effortlessly on thermal air currents, their eyes scanning the valley floor for their next meal. At my feet were new shoots of hardy perennials. It seemed to me that this primitive forest was strong and healthy, but I knew from Sidekick's lessons that this image was fragile, and the balance of nature delicate.

Fight, Famine, and Fire

S easons change rapidly in the river valleys. Winter moisture usually supplied the glacial reservoirs that kept streams cool well into the summer, but this year, the last month of summer became increasingly hot and dry. The lush green forest of the rain shadow turned into a parched environment. Animals were forced to increase the range of their search for food and water, leaving little time to shelter from the heat. These searches often brought animals into conflict over the dwindling food and water resources, providing us with several opportunities to put into practice the rules of Ravenwood.

Fir pitch is a nasty, sticky substance, almost impossible to remove from cat fur without leaving a bald spot. On a particularly hot morning, more than a year after I arrived in Ravenwood, I was working on the removal of pitch from my tender coat when I heard an alarm signal from Raven. Circling overhead and protesting vigorously, he plummeted below the ridge top and quickly ascended again. Repeatedly, I heard his call and saw him plunge. Thinking he was hunting, I continued what I was doing. In desperation, he flew directly at me, screaming as he passed by my ear. There was no mistaking what he meant—he needed me. I followed his ground shadow as I ran through the woods, feeling my rapid heartbeat in every artery and muscle. In my ears, my breath sounded more like a roar. The journey seemed to take forever with my short legs, and I was panting heavily as I dragged myself onto the rocky rim that provided a panoramic view of the area below.

In the shallow river, beneath a trickling waterfall, two bears were fighting: an aggressive black bear and a retreating Kodiak, twice as large. The black bear was using his sharp recurved claws to slash at the torso and hind legs of the Kodiak, which kept pushing him away and retreating. A Kodiak could outrun a horse for a short distance, but this bear was obviously injured to the point where it couldn't effectively fight or run. As I watched and did nothing, the Kodiak was quickly losing ground to its smaller but more fearsome opponent.

Tumbling more than running, I descended the ridge and ran along the riverbed, wondering how I could possibly help the victim. I reached the two wrestling bodies in time to witness the black bear gnashing at the neck of the other. With all my might, I leaped onto the black shoulder, burying my claws as deeply as I could into the tough hide, chomping down with locked jaw on tender ear tissue. With an anguished roar, he reared back and shook his head, trying to disengage my bite, but I held fast. He flung his head from side to side and swatted at his ear with his clawed paw until I released my bite and reinserted my teeth in a bald spot on the back of his neck, sending him rolling to the ground. I jumped out of his path. I continued to distract him, dodging back and forth, running between his legs, crouching and sprinting. Finally, bored with the chase, he wandered off into the woods.

Exhausted, I returned to the Kodiak that had dragged itself away from the fight scene to tend its wounds. As it raised its head to thank me, I realized the bear I had helped was Buddy. The fight was over a salmon that Buddy had caught, which was now lying on the rocky shore. I retrieved the fish for him and licked his wounds as he tried to regain his strength. Deeper than his physical wounds was the hurt he felt from the surprise attack by an overly aggressive bear. Losing a fight to a black bear was not the sort of thing one Kodiak could honorably discuss with another.

"Gosh, thanks, Topper, for helping me. I just don't know. I mean, gosh, what the heck happened to make him so angry? It was only a fish!"

"Don't worry about it," I said in an attempt to comfort him. "The fish must have been the last in a long line of events that went wrong for Blackie today. Extreme heat often makes an animal impatient. Are you in one piece?"

Buddy licked a few sore spots and confirmed that he would survive.

"It's embarrassing, you know, simply embarrassing! I mean, a big bear like me losing a tangle with a black bear. Gosh, the guys won't stop laughing until dawn."

His pride was injured, so, I stayed the night with Buddy. He needed someone to talk with. All night he replayed the fight, keeping the scars of his disgrace irritated, producing in him more fear and hopelessness. Listening to him, I realized how much greater damage mental injuries could cause than the quicker-healing physical wounds.

"It's all right, Buddy," I advised. "You didn't lose the fight, and you both survived another day."

At daybreak, he was still rehearsing what he should have done differently and questioning why it had happened. Unable to think of anything else to do for him, I just listened and listened and listened. By nightfall, he was beginning to tire of thinking about the event.

"We all live scarred lives," I said, "but the scars lose their pain when we live their lessons."

I paused in my explanation and shook my head. I was beginning to sound like my mother, and tears over her memory blurred my vision momentarily. Before Buddy noticed, I quickly removed their moisture with my left paw and continued explaining her words.

"A wise cat once told me that yesterday provides us with memories and hope, but it's up to us to understand the importance of each in our lives. Yesterday's battle may not leave a fond memory, Buddy, but your ability to survive it gives you all the hope you need for tomorrow."

I looked back over my shoulder to see if I had lost Buddy's interest. His droopy jaw had changed into a smile as he shook debris from his coat.

"Well, little fellow," he said, with renewed spirit, "you're not the same scared kitten that I first met. You're a full-grown thinker! You remind me a lot of Sidekick. Neither of you talks much, but when you do, it's sure worth listening."

After wishing Buddy well, I returned to the deer herd, walking around crevices in the dry soil that were several inches deep. Stream beds were shallow; no condensation was pooling anywhere in the forest. The parched earth made life difficult and dangerous for everyone. Young Buck suggested that Sidekick and I travel with him toward the ocean, where even neap tides infused the estuaries with nutrients. The salt water was not good for us to drink, but it supported life for vegetation and fish with its cyclic circulation.

Our journey to the ocean took us through the prairie dog coterie that, on this day, looked more like a ghost town. I scampered toward the mound I had first discovered a year earlier and noticed a female trying to stir her mate's limp body. She licked his face and shook his shoulders.

"Help me! Oh, help me!" she pleaded. "Marcus has fainted and I can't drag him inside."

She explained that Marcus had crossed the brown meadow looking for water in the hot sun, and dropped in his tracks before making it home. I gently grabbed the nape of his neck between my teeth, dragged his loose body to the mound, and lowered it into the hole. Millie pushed him into a cool lower chamber and returned topside with her sister, Mazie.

"Have you seen water anywhere?" they chimed in desperation.

Their mouths were dry, their tongues swollen, and they struggled against choking as they slurred their petition. Millie gave Mazie a reassuring kiss as they finished their plea. To their left, lying in a shaded pile of dry, needle-like grass, were their two surviving pups. I knew Mazie had birthed four of her own in the spring, and I could tell from the cracked and withered nipples on Millie that she had not fed a pup recently.

The two females stood together, pillars of stamina, supporting and embracing each other through this difficult time of tragedy with the remarkable courage of their convictions.

"We're going to get through this," affirmed Millie. "Every day that we survive, we beat the odds."

I looked toward the high mountains. The glacial reservoir had been receding all summer, and there was no sign of moisture on the lower slopes. Days of waning sunlight had already triggered seasonal changes in the deer, so there was hope that autumn's arrival would soon end this summertime drama.

"We haven't seen any water nearby, but we'll let you know what we find on our return route from the ocean," promised Young Buck.

"That's very kind of you." Millie sighed. "The pups haven't the energy to travel very far. We'll look for your return soon."

Along our day's journey, Sidekick and Young Buck foraged among the trees while I hunted for rodents seeking shelter from the sun. We knew when the ocean was close from the smell of ozone in the air and the reliable presence of gulls soaring overhead. They stalled and swooped as they scavenged the shoreline, fishing in flocks, chasing a fish from the path of one gull into the mouth of another. The thriving estuaries were unaware of the struggles of nature elsewhere. The sea food and timeless scenery were certainly rejuvenating.

Before returning to the mountains, Sidekick and I relaxed near the shore and watched as parent gulls demonstrated to their yearlings the precise art of dropping clams on rocks to crack open the shells. The two age groups were perfectly camouflaged: the white bodies of the adults against the billowy clouds, and the brown bodies of the young against the sand.

I watched as Young Buck walked along the tide's lacy edge toward an object in the water. Behind him, waves covered his hoof prints and receded, leaving no trace of his passage.

We all need waves in our lives, I thought, *to erase certain memories in our past and keep us headed forward.* How wonderful it would be if we could erase hurt from our minds as gently as the action of this tide erased hoof prints. So many truths in life seem to be coded and difficult to understand. Perhaps that's why Sidekick used metaphors and always seemed to be conjugating the air in an attempt to decode its meaning for me.

The sucking sound of another wave receding over a pebble beach alerted me to Young Buck's return. In his mouth he carried a shallow pan that had ridden a wave to shore. Plopping it down near Sidekick, he suggested they take turns carrying the pan, in which they could collect grass to take back to Millie.

The return trip was arduous and we stopped often, always remembering to collect any sprig of grass that had gone unnoticed by others. A few miles north of Millie's, we found a trickling stream. After much deliberation over how to keep the greens moist, I reluctantly twice drenched my fur and shook the drippings into the pan, where some of it was immediately absorbed.

When we arrived at Millie's, my fur was a frightful mess, but she was so ecstatic over the watered greens that I would have drenched myself again just for the pleasure of her smile. We watched as two struggling pups hydrated their bony bodies and cooled their faces in the residue of water.

A sip of this lifeblood did more than just restore them; it produced a remarkable change, as though they had endured a chrysalis state while their souls prepared to be butterflies. They danced and rolled and giggled between feasts, performing aerial waltzes as they jumped off logs. Fears of devastation were quelled; there was new hope for the future.

"It's remarkable, isn't it?" mused Young Buck.

"What is?" questioned Sidekick.

"I think it's remarkable that a simple gesture of kindness can relieve a distressed animal's fear and make room for peace and harmony to return."

That was the last time I saw the pups, but I'm confident that Millie's courage served them well until the next rain.

Our return trip to the lower mountains of Ravenwood was a pensive one after Sidekick explained why she felt privileged to live in the mountain forests of the gods.

"Except for a few non-natives," explained Sidekick, "the animals that live here today are fifth-generation descendants of parents who saved the forest when they were young. A sturdy, fun-loving, respectful group of animals that was willing to be surprised, not afraid of the unknown. They were not distracted by shadows in the night, but focused their attention on learning and understanding what could be seen in the light between the shadows. They were the great generation of code-breakers and code-talkers; a generation whose wisdom is lost in the elfin minds of today."

"Sidekick," I said gently. "You are a rare exception. You live a life of softened moments, simple and quiet in your thoughtful reserve. You turn situations into thoughts and break your silence only after you've broken their coded message."

"Topper's right," agreed Young Buck. "Sidekick moves through life with calm assurance, the way a bat maneuvers through a dark forest with its echolocation. She leaves the rest of us, with orphaned minds, curious and receptive, anxiously awaiting the benefit of her efforts."

"Nonsense!" stated Sidekick boldly. "You two praise too much."

"You are a rare treasure among all the animals I know," I contested. "How else can you explain your depth of knowledge and understanding?"

"My knowledge is the result of my training in observing and listening," explained Sidekick. "My parents and grandparents passed along great wisdom through their stories. When they died, it became my responsibility to continue the flow of knowledge to future generations. This is why I share my thoughts with you. You are part of my family. Through our actions, we might be able to prevent the repetition of previous tragedies."

"To what past tragedies are you referring?" asked Young Buck.

"It happened many generations ago," began Sidekick, "when humans introduced into our ecosystem non-native animals that disrupted the delicate balance and threatened the lives of all creatures along the food chain. Fragile alpine plants were destroyed when there was great competition for food and shelter among the native residents.

"Birds whose beaks were of different shapes and sizes so they wouldn't have to compete for the same foods were suddenly without the varieties they needed. Lepidoptera that fed on only one species of plant were devastated by its absence. The antlers of elk and deer failed to develop when their nutritional needs weren't met. Life was difficult and warring factions formed within herds, dividing a matriarchal society that once had been so strong. Total annihilation seemed imminent."

"What happened?" I asked, with great fascination.

"According to native legends, when all hope seemed lost and the animals were positioned, ready to attack each other, one young buck stepped forward and posed a question that changed the tide of events."

"What was the question?" asked Young Buck anxiously.

"In the early morning light, his question was answered to the satisfaction of all, and peace prevailed. That was the legacy of a great generation, and we are their heirs with an equally awesome task before us."

Nothing more was said as we each pondered the significance of Sidekick's story and our responsibility for the future. We wandered along until we found a lush green area. It was sheltered from the sun and fed by seepage from a spring that tapped retracting glacial flows. This oasis provided nourishment for all of us. I chased small prey through the grasses as the deer grazed. The challenging summer had left us all much leaner from the long walks and scarce food supply. We were grateful for every rejuvenating morsel found during the few softer days of fall, before the onslaught of winter that made us anxious for spring.

My next winter in Ravenwood slipped by uneventfully. I enjoyed the seasonal variation in landscape and food; I was more confident in the daily routines of the forest life, and comfortable with my family.

Deer, chasing each other around obstacles in the woods in early spring, are an enjoyable study in grace after the long, gray days of winter. These agile ruminants stretch their necks and shift their mass to the edge of their base, always ready to bolt if a protruding eye detects motion within the 310-degree range of their two-dimensional world. Partnered with Sidekick and an analytical raven, I had time to watch such playfulness and enjoy remembered salmon scents as I spent warm, lazy days catnapping.

On a sturdy branch in the treetop above me rested the largest nest in the woods, in which mated eagles took turns incubating three eggs. Every hour, the attending parent rotated the eggs and stretched its wings before settling back down on its warm feathered breast.

This was the second day that I had listened to an eaglet tap a rhythm on the shell that had protected it all month. In three months I would be watching its awkward flight lessons, but for now, I was anxious for the new arrival to complete its first task.

Raven, on the other hand, was busy rebuilding his own nest after yesterday's storm destroyed it in an apocalyptic whirlwind. Two by two, Raven carried branches in his mouth to a more sheltered tree, squawking at my laziness as he flew over and alerting his mate to his imminent arrival. Nothing distracted him from creating a home of geometric stability.

Looking around me, I could see the effects of nature's laws everywhere: centuries of pushing and pulling, lifting and dumping, freezing and melting. In my own acuity and blindness, the powers of Ravenwood reminded me that I was only a guest here for a catnap of infinity.

Crackle, crack, boom! A light over the next mountain flashed on my resting eyes. In the distance, a crackling crescendo stirred the forest, and a faint smell of smoke drifted overhead.

Raven halted his rebuilding project and took wing toward the sound. All faces of the forest were held at attention, awaiting word from the ridge. On rapid wing, Raven returned from surveying the situation. He stalled briefly and dipped one wing.

"Fire! Fire on the ridge! The wind is sending it here!" Suddenly I realized that I could understand Raven's words. His harsh, echoing caw was full of clear meaning.

I gasped and jumped to my feet. All around me there was panic. I looked up at the eagle nest and sadly realized that I would never watch the first flight lessons of the young birds, whose timing was too late for this world.

"Hmmm! Hmmmmmmmm! Hmmm!" cried the stray yearling, in anxious search of its mother.

The animals, racing through Ravenwood in flight from their burning homes, didn't notice the pleading of the youngster. Time passed rapidly. The smell of burning timber hovered in dark clouds above the treetops as heat from the raging fire grew more intense. The flames had jumped the adjacent ridge and were heading our way. Animals of every species that called this mountain home were running side by side with no predatory thought now. Hunger was their least concern. As they ran, they carried nothing with them except memories.

In this once peaceful corner of the world, the crashing sound of two-hundred-feet-tall conifers resonated through the hills. Gone were the treetop nests of birds and squirrels; gone were the burrows, dens, and thickets; gone were the meadows that had fed so many in this wilderness.

All afternoon, helicopters flew overhead, dumping huge buckets of water in man's best attempt to control the rage of nature, but to no avail. For a while, I could still see the river valley where I first met Buddy, and the high meadow where Sidekick became my mentor, but then smoke shrouded them both.

I watched as the fire raced across the switchback, not pausing to follow the lazy path that had brought me here when I was just a young cat. Thanks to the friends who had helped my life unfold here, I had grown wiser as well as older. Each experience added to my collection of adjectives for life, and I had lived life in full expression of them. So many young animals trapped between firebreaks would not be so fortunate.

Sidekick had shown me the destruction of the emerald green before, in the ghost forests near the west end. Branchless black-and-white trunks stood in the open as monuments to the past, before fire necessitated the evacuation of everything around them. It was a total destruction of life as it had been known. Trees, bushes, grasses, mosses—everything that lived and gave life was gone. It was a landscape bereft, with tannin-colored streams clogged by so much debris that no salmon could return to spawn. The ground was covered with such an abundance of slash and stumps that no deer, bear, or elk could traverse such wreckage.

Ravenwood was more than just a home to me; it was a daily inspiration. The sights, sounds, and smells that greeted each breath gave purpose to everything that followed.

"What are you going to do?" asked Sidekick, flicking her tall ears at me. "You can't stay here any longer. The fire is too close."

"I don't know," I sobbed. "It's hard enough to be forced to leave Ravenwood, but to see it completely destroyed is unbearable. I can't take it."

In silence, we stood on the grassy knoll in Ravenwood, my mentor and I. Sidekick licked the fur behind my ear and reminded me of what she had advised years ago.

"Topper, my friend," she said. "Ravenwood is more than just a place; it is a way of life. When you leave, you can take it with you. It can exist anywhere."

Even in the face of all this devastation, Sidekick spoke with unhurried peace. I searched the ember's glow for a sign of hope. Ravenwood had survived forces of calamity before. Maybe it could withstand fire too.

"Sidekick," I pleaded. "Who was the young buck that saved the great generation? Do you know?"

"Yes," she replied. "He was my great-great-grandfather."

"What was the question he asked?"

"It is a question that saves us from ourselves: from our own fear and apathy; from outrage and discouragement; from sorrow and pain."

"What was the question?" I reiterated frantically.

Sidekick turned slowly and faced the young river beds near the ocean.

"He asked 'Which way is forward?'" she said, with conviction.

The fury of the fire raged in my ears. Soon there would be nothing left in the forest to define the wind or hush the rain. It would be vacant of the bright green new growth, but not of hope. Through its eternal resilience, the green would someday return, but not in my lifetime.

Already, in the few years of my existence, I had experienced the sorrow of separation from my mother and Maggie, the loss of the cousins and my tail. And now, after discovering the universal fraternity of all living things in the rules of Ravenwood, it seemed, I would lose Ravenwood too.

"Our footprints here are only temporary," explained Sidekick. "Ravenwood is not the mountains, trees, and flowers. It is not the valleys, streams, or mist. It is their perpetual fragrance. That intangible, fragrant memory is with you always, instantly recalling for you all the memories of your love."

Overhead, on upward wing, flew Raven, beckoning me to follow him into the next phase of my life, more knowledgeable and hopeful than before, but still with Sidekick at my side.

Ravenwood

Follow the River

New Beginnings

It was dusk when a warm, steady breeze led us away from the raging fire in Ravenwood. Relentlessly, it compelled us forward as we attempted to leave our sadness behind in dream-like memories. Ravenwood, and the lessons learned in its lush forests, snowcapped mountains, glacial rivers, and abundant wildlife, would live on in each animal that had called it home.

"Which way should we go?" I asked as we wearily made our way through the forest.

"Follow the river! Follow the river!" advised Raven as he soared overhead.

"The river knows the way forward," explained Sidekick. "It will lead us to the safety of a lower mountain meadow."

"But where are Tiny and the others?" I asked.

"Tiny and her friends were foraging near the switchback when the fire broke out. They probably escaped down the eastern side of the mountain."

With regretful eyes, I shook my head in disgust as I looked back toward the fire that was devastating the once-green paradise.

"What a waste! A terrible waste of beauty and goodness," I exclaimed.

Plodding along the hard-beaten path of animals fleeing in front of me, I noticed that Sidekick's body seemed lined with pain.

"Don't let the vision fade. Burning trees only challenge our lives. Right now we must consider our present possibilities. "

Sidekick spoke of the present, but I knew she also felt a sense of loss. I closed my eyes in the pale daylight and listened to the cry of the wind that fueled the burning rage of the conifer branches. Ravenwood would be dated by this event, just as its trees had been dated by droughts. The tree rings would document the history of events in the forest; its lessons would continue to be a guiding force in the future.

The forest before us was darkening quickly as we traveled beneath the old conifers. Behind us, the sky was ablaze with sparks rising from the treetops. Up, up, up they climbed until cooler air dimmed their glow and returned them to earth. My throat was irritated from heavy panting in the smoke-filled air as I tried my best to keep up with Sidekick's rapid descent. Finally, we paused at the river, where a cool rock provided a clear spot for a touch-up bath. I tried to remove the smoky scent from my fur, but my saliva wasn't sufficient for the task.

"We need to cross the river soon," said Sidekick anxiously. "It gets deeper and wider the farther down we follow it. Soon it will become too difficult for us to cross."

"Cross the river! Are you serious?" I exclaimed. "I don't like water! Nope, I'm not crossing the river. Water is good for fish, but not for cats. We'll just have to live on this side of the river."

"We have no choice, Topper. The fire is continuing to advance. The river will act as a firebreak. There are only a few trees on the other riverbank, so the flames can't easily jump across. We'll be safe over there. You must try, Topper. Let your trust in me be greater than your fear."

In the dark, I could hear the sound of rapids beating against the river rocks as we proceeded along the edge. I didn't know what Sidekick had in mind, but I knew I could trust her judgment.

"Over here, Topper! Beyond the bend, where the river flows straight for a while. The water depth and speed should not change much here."

The crossing point that Sidekick had chosen resembled a gauntlet of rocks, logs, and rapids. I began studying the possibilities. Perhaps I could use a fallen tree as a bridge to the sandbar in the middle of the river. Then I would have to jump from one rock to another over rapids to reach the other side. I licked my right paw and rubbed behind my ear for a while. Next, I pulled on each claw with my teeth, testing their individual strength. Slowly I walked to the end of the fallen tree, reached up with my front feet, and sharpened each set of claws until the bark of the tree was nearly shredded. Hopping on top of the fir bridge, I began my precarious journey across the river. Sidekick waded next to me on the downstream side.

"Can't I just ride across on your back?" I pleaded with Sidekick.

"No, Topper. You must learn to cross a river under your own power in case I'm not with you sometime when it is necessary for you to do this. Don't look down, Topper. Focus on your destination and you should do fine."

I didn't know how Sidekick knew the proper technique of tree walking, but then I didn't know how Sidekick had come to know much of what she knew. I just heeded her advice and walked slowly in a crouched position to the end of the tree. In the dark forest, noises were exaggerated. The hot breeze and raging rapids roared in my ears. I could see the faint outline of the first rock. The surface looked flat, but I knew it was probably slimy as well. How I wished I had my long tail for balance! My claws wouldn't be much help on a slippery rock.

"You can do it, Topper. I know you can," Sidekick encouraged me.

I looked at the rock and estimated the amount of spring required to reach that destination. Too much or too little would mean a cold drowning in the glacial waters. I had to be precise.

"I have to do this!" I told myself. "I have no other choice. If I don't hurry, Sidekick's legs will get too cold and she will become weakened. I must do this n-n-n-ow!"

With cat-like grace, I sprang through the air over the first rapid, landed squarely on the rock, and slid to a halt.

"Good for you, Topper. Only three rocks left."

I accepted Sidekick's praise and evaluated the next three rocks. They were considerably smaller with bursts of water rushing over them most of the time.

"You'll have to take the next set together," warned Sidekick. "You'll only have time to touch and leap between rocks. If you land and pause, the water bursts will knock you downstream."

I observed the timing of the rapid splashes on each rock and realized they were without pattern. My first jump would have to be downstream, at an angle. Upon landing, I would need to make a quarter turn, and immediately leap upstream to the next rock; turn again toward shore, and leap to the final rock. Then I would have only a moment to pause before jumping three feet to the gravel shore, and safety.

I recited this strategy to myself as I took on the challenge and completed the first set. Then I was shocked by *i–i–i–i–cy water*! Just as I started my last leap toward shore, an unexpected burst of water crested the last rock and drenched my long coat. I shook off the wetness before making my final jump to safety.

The cold from my drenching lingered long into the night. Sidekick tried to keep me warm, snuggled against her body, but the glacial waters had chilled me to the bone. I couldn't stop shivering. All night long I struggled to preserve my body heat. My tongue was tired from constantly licking my fur in an attempt to fluff it enough to allow it to air dry.

Morning broke early on the edge of the meadow, where no trees obstructed the smoky sunlight. Thirst had awakened me. I made my way across the field to a large depression where water had collected. Just as I began to drink, I heard Sidekick shout for me to stop. I immediately withdrew my tongue from the stagnant pool and asked Sidekick why I wasn't allowed to quench my thirst.

"We don't know this area, Topper. We haven't observed it long enough to know if the still water is safe to drink. It could be contaminated by feces or larvae that could make you sick. We don't know when it last rained in this meadow. You'd better stick to drinking moving water until we learn differently."

I thanked her for the warning and followed her back to the riverbed. Sidekick waded in a few feet for her drink, and I drank upstream along the edge of the river, which was covered in the night tracks of raccoons and other thirsty wildlife.

Flies, which hovered over the water, swarmed maliciously around my head. I swatted frantically at each one, and their occasional demise by the action of my paw provided only temporary relief. I looked over at Sidekick and watched as the pests circled her dream-widened eyes.

"What are you thinking?" I asked as I took another sip of water.

There was no response, so I did not further disturb her silence with my thoughts. Quietly, I reminded myself of the rules of Ravenwood: first, notice everything; second, do no harm; and third, own nothing.

Sidekick said that we should take these rules with us wherever we went.

I stepped away from the river, looking around me. The snowcapped mountains were still clearly visible with their irregular ridges. The smell of smoke was pungent in the air. The stream water was no longer clear, and it tasted of tannin from fallen trees. Overhead, Raven repeated his sonorous cry of sadness and separation. I watched, listened, and breathed with greater acuity than ever before as I waited for Sidekick to break her silence.

In our search for a new home, the rules of Ravenwood would definitely play an important role to help us find just the right place: a place where we felt a sense of belonging and purpose. Along the journey, we would need to be careful to do no harm, leaving only the smallest imprint of our passage.

"It's time to go," Sidekick stated. She headed toward the forest with timid caution. She paused between each measured stride, listening, scanning, and sniffing. Even ant trails didn't go unnoticed. Obediently, I stayed downwind of her exceptional senses and remained quiet. I realized that our hurried exodus from the ancient mountains of Ravenwood had become a cautious odyssey into its lowlands.

Another day passed. We continued our journey through the lower forest. Sidekick nibbled on the new growth of cedar branches that provided a pleasant shade for us. I dined on exhausted shrews that I outchased. Above us, a sapsucker hammered its way around a tree, its beak left perforated paths in its search for food. From behind us, we could still hear the sound of the river rushing toward the sea, but there was also an unnatural silence before us. I removed a burr from my shoulder. Sidekick slowed her gait, flicked her tail, and examined prints in the packed soil.

"Are we in danger? That print looks rather large," I commented. I placed my paw beside a much larger version of its shape.

"Not from this cougar," explained Sidekick. "He's long gone."

"How can you tell? He could be waiting for us beyond those logs."

"Not likely. This print is two days old. Take a closer look at its details."

I sniffed the print and examined its contents and shape.

"Well, inside the obvious print of a cougar, all I see is a pressed alder leaf that appears to be dry and crumbly. How do you know the print was made two days ago?"

"Because, Topper, yesterday and today have been sunny, and the only heavy dew we've had recently was on the morning of the fire. The cougar left this print after the dew, when the soil was moist, and the moist leaf was pressed into its shape. The sun dried the leaf, and nothing else has fallen in the print since then."

"How do you know this leaf didn't fall there after a rain?"

"Because a rain would have washed away the hard edges of the print."

"Oh." I sighed. "What about the print tells you that the cat is no longer a threat to us?"

Sidekick walked along the path of prints and explained. "The stride length tells me that the cougar was running. We haven't come across any scratches or fecal markings that the cougar would have used to identify its territory, so it was probably just passing through, escaping the fire like the rest of us."

There seemed to be no end to Sidekick's depth of knowledge. She was a deep well of certainty. I observed her with awed respect all day as she traveled against the wind, backtracked, and then found a resting place where the wind could warn her of an approaching predator. From her chosen spot, she could view the most vulnerable area, across the wind.

"The wind in these lower forests is different," I remarked to Sidekick. "The breeze seems quieter and in less of a hurry."

"Down here there are no mountain peaks to block the path of the wind, so it isn't forced to travel quickly between peaks and scream its intent," replied Sidekick. "With fewer obstructions, the wind is free to enter the valley as a gently ushered breeze."

Scratching my ear in an attempt to scare away a few pesky flies, I asked, "How much farther before we get to our new home?"

"I don't know," responded Sidekick.

"Will we be there tomorrow?"

"I don't know."

"Well, where is this new place?"

"I don't know that either."

"Then how will we know when we've arrived?"

"We'll just know," Sidekick assured me.

"But what if we get separated? What if I get lost? How will I know where to find the right place?"

"When we find the right place, we'll both recognize it. Don't worry; you'll be all right," replied Sidekick, with a big yawn followed by a few shallow coughs.

She looked more tired than I had ever seen her before. I was concerned that leaving Ravenwood was taking more of a toll on her than I had previously realized. She needed a rest, a long rest, before we continued our journey.

I kept watch as Sidekick slipped into a dream. Her nose had the long, gradual curve of her ancestry that equally divided the benign expression on her face. She had no illusions about life. Her mind contemplated possibilities and seldom spent time reprising past events. I hoped the faces that we would meet in the new forest would be as pleasant as hers.

Long ribbons of sunlight streaked the few visible clouds on this butterfly day. Birds searched for overlooked seeds among the twigs. A squirrel peeled bark and moss from a cedar branch above me to line its nest. Earlier it had been chattering, but now its mouth was full on each trip up the tree. Today, the sky was blown clean by the wind. Only a hint of smoke remained from the tragedy of Ravenwood.

Sidekick had taught me to use the wind as a compass, as it often didn't change much in one day. I checked the direction of the wind, and then looked around for indications of previous activity. The grass to the west of us was marked with a green stripe. The blades weren't bent, but I knew this stripe indicated a recent trail, because the sunlight had marked it a different shade of green. I wondered if Sidekick would follow this phantom path or head in a different direction.

"Get up! Get up! Get up!" called Raven as he approached for a landing. "What's the matter with you two? You're sleeping away the daylight. Aren't you anxious to find a new home?"

Raven was right. We had lazed away a good part of the day. It was time to be making tracks of our own.

"Let me grab a bite to eat. Then we'll be on our way again," stated Sidekick.

I pounced on an area where the grass was four times my height and suggested that Sidekick feast on it.

"No, thanks," she replied. "We're on the windward side of our mountain now, and the grass on this side grows so rapidly that it can't absorb many nutrients before the rain leaches them from the soil. I'll browse the shrubs over there."

Raven and I spent our time hunting for mice and moles while Sidekick nibbled on selected leaves and seedlings. Soon, Sidekick put her nose to the wind, and we were off on our journey again.

Sidekick could walk through a forest maze as though it were not there. Normally, she traveled as effortlessly as a shadow, but again today she seemed weary as she looked for signs of warning and welcome.

"There's a place for everything," she kept mumbling. "A place for everything."

Her breathing was labored, and I didn't ask her to elaborate on what she meant. I noticed an erratic motion in the ferns and was about to make mention of it when a fumbling yearling emerged.

"H-h-hello," he stuttered. "M-m-my name is T-T-Tanner!"

"Hello, Tanner," responded Sidekick graciously. "We're looking for a new home. I hope we didn't disturb you. Can you tell us about this area where you live?"

"Oh, I-I-I don't l-l-live here," he replied sheepishly. "I-I-I just m-m-move about. The a-a-animals don't l-l-let me s-s-stay anywhere v-v-very long."

How sad, I thought. I noticed the sway in Tanner's weakened frame, and how his eyes oozed sticky mucus. This poor creature had no home, no family, and no friends to care for him.

"What good luck!" exclaimed Sidekick, much to my astonishment. "We're all looking for the same thing! We might as well look together, if it's all right with you."

"S-s-sure!" replied Tanner excitedly. "I-I-I'll show y-y-you around a-a-a bit."

For the rest of the afternoon, we slowly followed Tanner through the wooded acreage. Raven became impatient with our pace and flew ahead to survey the area. As nightfall approached, Tanner led us to a hillside stripped of trees. Exposure had eroded the ravine and made traversing it uncertain and difficult. Beyond the wreckage, we found a protected area suitable for resting.

"Sidekick?" I asked, as we settled in for the night "Why did you say Tanner was lucky? It seems to me that he has had nothing but bad luck, being rejected from every place he travels."

"I wasn't saying that just Tanner was lucky. I think that we were all lucky to meet at that place and time. How do we know if what happened to Tanner in the past was bad luck? Sometimes things just happen; they are not always about bad luck or good luck. What is important is the way we handle the things that happen to us. Life is a journey that can't be summarized until you reach the end."

The tone of Sidekick's voice was kind but firm. She alone would define her life, and she reserved this individual right for everyone else too.

"The very experience that you term bad luck may lead Tanner into his next fortunate experience. It's all a part of the story of life." Sidekick yawned.

"What do you mean? What is the story of life?" I inquired.

"I'm too tired to explain it all now, but I'll leave you with this thought for the night: that which makes an animal odd in one environment, actually gives him or her an advantage in another. The challenge in life is to find the environment for which you are best suited. Once you have found it, thrive and be happy."

Sidekick was fast asleep, but I was wide awake thinking about what she had said. Every loss in my life had led me into a new experience. The loss of my mother and siblings led me to Maggie; Maggie brought me to Ravenwood; in Ravenwood I met Sidekick; and now the fire in Ravenwood had set us on a journey to find a new home. Perhaps Sidekick was correct. Maybe luck was considered good or bad depending on where you were on life's story line.

"Hey, T-T-Topper," whispered Tanner. "Are you c-c-cold?"

I left Sidekick's warm body and snuggled next to Tanner's shaking belly.

"Maybe we can stay warm together," I said as I tucked my head between my paws. I looked over at Sidekick in time to see her flash me a wink.

For the next several days I kept pace with Tanner while Raven and Sidekick led us down the mountainside.

"So, T-T-Topper, were you b-b-born in t-t-these mountains?"

"Not hardly," I replied. "I was born in an animal shelter next to a cornfield. Just about the time I was learning to enjoy life with my siblings, I was adopted by Maggie, who brought me to this mountain country. She was killed in a fire the first night we arrived."

"H-h-how did you m-m-meet Sidekick and R-R-Raven?"

"That's a story I'll never forget! You see, I was hungry after Maggie died, so I started chasing a large bird from tree to tree. I was climbing a tree when I heard Sidekick's voice below me ask what I was doing. After I told her I was hunting, she introduced me to Raven, whom I'd been chasing, and suggested that I follow her to a place where I could catch fish for my meal. I agreed, and we've been together ever since. What about you? Where were you born?"

"I-I-I don't r-r-really recall, j-j-just somewhere up t-t-that mountain," he said as he turned and faced the mountain behind us. "I-I-I've been m-m-moving down t-t-that mountain ever s-s-since."

"Hey!" I exclaimed, noticing that Sidekick was moving out of sight. "We'd better hurry before we get too far behind."

"Ah, I-I-I never h-h-hurry."

"Why not? Are you too sick?"

"N-n-no, I'm j-j-just afraid."

"Afraid of what?"

"D-d-don't know w-w-where to g-g-go when I r-r-reach the b-b-bottom."

"We can't worry about that now. We need to stay close to the others."

A long sprint put us within sight of Sidekick, where once again I felt it safe to continue conversing with Tanner.

"Why does everyone chase you away?"

"T-t-they say I'm d-d-different."

"We're all different. Why is that a reason?"

"T-t-they don't n-n-need a r-r-reason, j-j-just an excuse!"

I looked up at Tanner and swatted at several flies circling his low-hanging head. Flies always attack the individual too weak to brush them away, and they keep circling until they can overtake the animal. I pretended it was a game. I let him think that I swatted at the pests for my own enjoyment.

The following day, Tanner and I walked so close together that our breath clouds mingled. I pounced at dew diamonds and he dragged his legs across the open meadow. By nightfall, his eyes were almost sealed shut with mucus. I gently licked the eyelids of his bulging brown eyes until they were temporarily clear.

"Would you like to hear a story?" asked Sidekick.

"Oh, p-p-please do t-t-tell us a s-s-story."

"What story will you tell?" I asked her.

"I will tell you the story of life that my mother told me. A long time ago, along the northern shore, grew a gigantic species of flowers. The rain and sunshine provided them with deep roots and tall stalks. Each year, the seeds grew more plentiful until finally there were more seeds than space allowed along the shoreline for so many to grow so tall. The growth of some flowers was stunted in the shade of taller ones. These shorter-stalked flowers became fuzzy and wider, and were harassed by the swaying of the taller ones all season long. But at the end of each season, they too let the wind of change spread their seeds. Eventually, the winds carried the seeds of the small, fuzzy flowers up the mountain to a cold, windy environment for which they were perfectly adapted. On the shoreline, the small flowers were starved for sunlight. Likewise, in the mountains, the tall flowers were broken by the winds."

Sidekick paused, and then looked directly into the tearful eyes of Tanner.

"Each species, no matter how different, thrives in its proper place, but sometimes an individual isn't born in the place best suited for its survival. Its life journey, therefore, is to search for a place where it can flourish and be happy. Everything has its proper place, Tanner, and we will help you find yours."

For the next few days, Tanner seemed to be in better spirits. His pace quickened when he was no longer afraid to reach the bottom of the mountain. He seldom spoke of animals who had chased him in the past. He continued to ask me about my adventures in the forest. I taught him the rules of Ravenwood and the life lessons I had learned there.

During our third week together, Tanner developed an uncontrollable cough. Each bout seemed to weaken him, and as he tried to clean himself, more hair fell from his body. His alopecia left very little insulation, allowing the cold drafts to attack his lungs.

"I don't know what to do to help him," I said to Sidekick. "The fur on my body isn't enough to cover the hairless area on him."

"It's all right, Topper. Don't worry about what you can't do. Just do for him all that you can. It will be enough."

"But he's getting worse, not better! How can you say it's enough?" My eyes overflowed with tears and I felt an anxious ache in my throbbing heart.

"Because he has good luck, not bad."

"Good luck? Good luck?" I questioned loudly. "Tanner is dying! He has no home, no family, no future! Nothing good has happened to him in his entire life, which is almost over, and you still insist that he is lucky?"

Sidekick studied me.

"You happened, Topper. You are what made a difference in his life. You took an interest in him. You let him know how much you care. You shared with him the best part of you. No matter what else happens, you gave him a good experience to take with him. A life of good memories is all that really matters in your fifth season. So what if you can't stop his cough or the loss of his hair? If you are doing whatever you can to make him happy, it is enough. We are each entitled to good luck and a gentle resolution."

I felt powerless to improve Tanner's situation, but Sidekick's words eased my mind. Nothing I could do would change his past or meet all of his needs, but I was willing to do whatever I could to make this moment pleasant for him.

"What's the fifth season? I thought there were only four," I asked of Sidekick.

"You'll discover it soon enough, and then you'll understand."

I walked over to where Tanner was resting, to tell him it was time for us to move along. He rose to his feet, shook himself, stumbled, and started walking with determination toward a patch of wildflowers.

"Who, who, who! Who who!" drew my attention to a cedar branch worn smooth from a perching barred owl. Sidekick walked toward the tree and struck up a conversation with the large striped bird.

"Good morning, Owl," began Sidekick.

"Good morning to you, little lady. I don't recall seeing you in these woods before."

"We're just passing through on our way down the mountain. Have you any news for us to take along?"

"Passing through, you say? There seems to be quite a bit of that going on recently. Have you, by any chance, come from Ravenwood?"

Sidekick looked surprised as she affirmed that we had.

"Just last week, I met a doe with a pair of scrawny fawns falling all over themselves. I suppose you'll know what that's like soon enough." He chuckled. "They spent a few days in a fern patch beyond that hill while the youngsters got adjusted. I don't remember her name, but she said she had left Ravenwood when the fire jumped the ridge."

"Do you remember anything about her? What did she look like?" I asked.

"Well, now, let me see. She seemed a bit forlorn; had a bum leg, as I remember, but certainly was patient with those youngsters. Kept looking back over her shoulder, like she was expecting someone to follow. She told a sad story, she did, all about the fire, and the eagles losing the eggs in their nests, and her friends frantically escaping the heat and flames. An awful tragedy, it was. I'm so sorry you were forced to leave. The doe described it as a wonderful place to live." Owl looked directly at Sidekick now. "I suppose you'll need to find a place to live real soon, if you'll pardon my presumption."

I had no idea what Owl meant by some of his comments to Sidekick, but I was delighted to know that friends had passed this way ahead of us. Perhaps Matie was the doe that Owl had seen. She had broken her leg years ago, and sometimes it still bothered her. I hoped we would be able to join up with her in a few days.

"Thank you for your concern, Owl, but could you describe for us the land and animals beyond the hill?"

"Absolutely, little darling. I'd be happy to help you."

Owl spread his wings and floated to a lower branch to give Sidekick's neck a rest from looking up all the time.

"In this forest, beyond that sentinel line of cedars, we have a world rich in everything you could desire: lichens, brush, mosses, liverworts, and grasses. Our stream is blessed with sockeye salmon, which your cat would enjoy, but it is heavily hunted by other animals that its protein supports. Also, our restless riverbed tends to flood every available inch of ground during the winter rains. It might be too difficult a life for someone as precious as you."

"Thank you, Owl. We certainly appreciate your advice. Happy hunting!"

"My pleasure, little darling. Good luck to you along your way."

I also thanked Owl for the news and chuckled at his wishing good luck to Sidekick. Good luck was the only luck she ever accepted.

Various types of mosses softened the rugged contours of the cedars and firs as we threaded our way through the next forest. Bracket fungus attached to the same trees where woodpeckers frantically hammered out rhythms, classifying the trees as doomed from disease. Beyond the forest, we walked through a meadow where the grass had been flattened, apparently, by a large herd of resting elk. The area appeared to be hospitable to life, but I trusted Sidekick's instinct to move on.

Evening found us so quickly that I was disappointed we hadn't made better progress closing the gap between us and our Ravenwood companions. Tanner's voice sounded brittle from so much coughing, so we didn't spend much time talking that night. I was restless from anticipation, but I finally fell asleep to the distant sound of Owl defending his territory from invaders.

"Where'd he go? Where'd he go?" repeated Raven frantically as he hopped up and down on the ground next to me the following morning. "Where's Tanner?"

I arched my stiff back and slithered quickly into a half stretch as I noticed that Sidekick was also missing.

"He must be lost. That's it," repeated Raven. "He's wandered off, and now Sidekick has gone in search of him. I'll take to the sky, and you follow my shadow."

"Will do! Let me know as soon as you see them."

I bounded over branches and waded through ferns, following the most direct route of Raven's shadow in the temporary bursts of sunlight between trees. Dried leaves rustled underfoot as I rushed below the high canopy of alders. Above me, Raven was now circling the treetops.

"What are you doing?" I yelled.

"Searching for a scent."

"Whose scent? I didn't know you could distinguish one animal scent from another."

"I can't," he replied, "but I can detect methane if it's present. Dead animals release methane gas as their carcasses decay."

"Raven! Stop saying those things. They haven't been gone very long. Search for live animals!"

"All right, but you have to admit that it's a possibility. Tanner is getting weaker every day. It's going to happen sometime."

I couldn't believe how depressing Raven still was after knowing Sidekick as long as he had. Sidekick would never accept such diversions, and neither would I. She would tell me to keep my eye on the goal and not let anything distract me. Discouragement, she had once warned, was the biggest distraction of all.

"Do you see anything yet, Raven? Any sign that they came this way?"

"I see a bobcat chasing a rabbit, and a coyote dropping some scat, but that's about it. You rest on that stump and I'll fly higher."

I was ready for a breather after such a fast pace through the woods. Where could Tanner and Sidekick have gone in such a short time? Neither one had moved very quickly the past few days. Perhaps we were traveling in the wrong direction. Maybe they were headed against the wind.

"There! There!" pointed Raven, with a dipped wing.

I hurried down a hill that was much farther north of the direction in which we had been headed. As I approached a small clearing, I met Tanner and Sidekick walking back toward me.

"Where have you been?" I shouted as they approached. "Tanner, you shouldn't run off like that. It's dangerous to walk about by yourself."

"I-I-I know," replied Tanner. "T-t-that's why I-I-I left."

"You've made a wrong assumption, Topper," explained Sidekick. "I didn't follow him; he followed me."

"T-t-that's right, T-T-Topper. I-I-I saw her l-l-leave, and d-d-didn't think s-s-she s-s-should be alone. W-w-we thought y-y-you'd find us s-s-sooner."

"We probably would have, had we known you were following instead of leading." I laughed.

Sidekick was right about the trouble with making wrong assumptions and trying to figure out things that never happened. I recalled her telling me a story about a sly squirrel trying to escape a predator. He slipped into the large opening of a hollow log and concealed himself there for quite a long time. At least, most of him was concealed. Part of his bushy tail actually protruded from a very small hole on top of the log. A group of small forest animals had gathered around the log to contemplate how such a large squirrel squeezed through such a small hole. The circumstance, as Sidekick told it, was laughable. I think she must have known I would recall the situation when she mentioned wrong assumptions. In my laughter, I forgot to ask Sidekick why she had ventured off, but I supposed her reason didn't matter anymore. All of us were together again, heading down the mountain.

Since leaving Ravenwood, we had not strayed far from the river. At its pristine headwaters, the river was slight and narrow, but it fell forcefully as it descended the mountain. In these lowlands, the broadening river was now keeping pace with us.

When we began our journey, the Indian plum was not yet in color in the high terrain. We descended the mountain and met Tanner on our way to the low meadows where the skunk cabbage showed its bright yellow stalks. Owl we met when the coltsfoot bloomed. The rich scent of cedars, fractured by winter winds, still filled the air as I looked back toward Ravenwood to see what new sculpture the melting glaciers had formed. Around us, in contrast, the spring flowers made a patchwork of these meadows below the forest line. At that moment, the sun was clearly visible at its zenith, but it wouldn't be for much longer. Moving quickly across the sky were dark clouds ready to burst.

"The air seems thick today," commented Sidekick breathlessly. "It's difficult to breathe in this humid heat."

"The approaching rain should cool us off. I think we should seek shelter, though, for Tanner's sake."

Normally, a deer wouldn't be concerned about a northwest rain, but Tanner had no hair to repel the water, and the cool rain would chill his bones. Sidekick smiled in Tanner's direction and agreed we needed to find shelter soon.

We left the forest and had traveled halfway across the lea when the cloud I had been watching burst, showering us with its cold dampness.

"Any sign of shelter, Raven?" I shouted.

"There's an old barn over the next rise. It should offer protection. I'll meet you there."

As Tanner was having difficulty walking on the softened soil, I stayed close enough to encourage him. Sidekick walked on ahead and managed to kick the broken barn door open wide enough for Tanner to wobble through.

"W-w-what a relief to f-f-find such a n-n-nice shelter!"

The vacated barn smelled of soured hay, rotten wood, moldy hemp ropes, and rats. It was pleasantly warm and relatively dry in the northeast corner, where some of the roof material remained in place. When I searched the area for food, I found a nearly empty bin of grain that had been breached by, what else, rats! Below the opening of the grain bin was a tunnel that ran across the floor to the other side of the barn. The smell of rats was pervasive. Sidekick claimed that she was more tired than hungry, preferring to rest first and eat later. Tanner also agreed. Knowing the loathsome nature of rats, I kept watch over the food supply while my friends rested.

It wasn't long before I heard the scurrying sound of rat feet approaching the bin. I adjusted my stance and pounced on its head as the rat exited the tunnel.

"Ye-oow!" screamed Rat. "Get off of me, you home invader!"

"I'm sorry we invaded your home, but it's only temporary. We just need shelter from the rain and a small amount of food."

"Listen, you thunderhead, I have no intention of being your dinner, small or otherwise!"

"You don't have to be my dinner, Rat. Just leave enough grain for my two friends. They have lost a lot of strength on our journey and need to share your food supply."

"From the looks of that hairless weakling, he should be my dinner soon. How about you leave him here in exchange for a meal of grain for the other one?"

"No deal, Rat! We'll all go hungry before we make a deal like that. Now, are you willing to share your grain, or do I have to bat you around a bit?"

"All right! All right! Your friends can have some grain, but it will be wasted on the weak one. Now turn me loose!"

Reluctantly, I released my grip on my catch of the day. I had eaten well yesterday and seemed to be managing better on our journey than either Tanner or Sidekick. With an agreed deal, I felt secure in catching a catnap and reviewing pleasant memories.

The sun had passed over the barn when I jumped from my sleep at the sound of Raven swooping down across me. Suddenly, Tanner screamed, and Sidekick bolted from her resting place. Raven had seen Rat approach Tanner, and had swooped down and caught him, but not before Rat had taken a small bite out of Tanner's hip.

"You gluttonous, lying creep! You promised! I trusted you!" I yelled.

"What did you expect, you fool? It's a rat's instinct to eat everything in sight. I just took a little taste! I haven't eaten live venison before!"

"It's not instinct, it's greed and deception," I rebuked him. "You're no better than a snake that hides its venom and intent."

"What do you want me to do with him, Topper?" inquired Raven.

"I think you have every right to eat him to put an end to his nefarious motives, but the decision is up to Tanner. What do you think, Tanner?"

"W-w-what good w-w-would it do t-t-to eat him? Are y-y-you hungry R-R-Raven?"

"Not really. I filled up earlier today."

"Then b-b-better do no h-h-harm, Topper. G-g-give him a c-c-chance to r-r-redeem himself. T-t-turn him l-l-loose."

Sidekick smiled at Tanner's application of the second rule of the forest and nodded in my direction. Raven immediately dropped Rat (not gently) into the mouth of the rat tunnel and returned to a perch.

We remained long enough for Tanner and Sidekick to eat a light meal of grain, and for me to watch a spider construct a durable web from its delicate gossamer strands. But not even that phenomenon could take my mind off of Rat's disgusting mouth. Everything about him disgusted me. I didn't have Tanner's hope that Rat would change because I had always known rats to be neophobic. They were afraid of change, of anything new, always following the same paths. As totally predictable creatures, they were easy to catch.

The rain that led us to seek shelter also brought to my attention the activity of slugs and snails that normally relied on their own mucus secretions to slide across the dry earth. When the sun returned, so did the sublime butterflies that carefully flew close to the ground, so as not to get caught in a breeze that would carry them beyond the range of the Indian thistle that fed their nervous motion. Eagles soared overhead in a clear sky. They rode updrafts of warm air from lower elevations to the cooler air of mountain peaks. This region of the forest, like others beyond the reach of man's influence, was an unweeded garden in the study of life.

According to Sidekick, nature provided a selection of opposites from which to choose a course of action, and made clear the consequences of each choice. An ethical animal may know the difference between right and wrong action, but a moral animal chooses to demonstrate the right action in his or her daily life. To Sidekick, there was no point in professing an understanding of rules or standards if an animal had no intention of living in accordance with those values.

I was glad that Tanner had chosen to spare the life of Rat. It's not always easy to forgive those who have hurt you, especially when the wound is still fresh. I recalled my earlier encounter with Ba-soht and Ka-newk and realized that, by forgiving them, I felt empowered with a sense of freedom. We never reconciled as friends because what happened still mattered; it was wrong. But forgiving them released me from perpetuating the suffering I had experienced, from the pain they had caused. An apology would have been nice, quickening my willingness to forgive, but it wasn't required for me to move beyond that experience. Sidekick had said that a bad experience is as harmless as passing through a grove of rotten hemlocks: it isn't dangerous unless you stay too long and the wind uproots them.

Ahead of me, Sidekick and Tanner were standing by a pool of water trapped by a sandbar at the side of the river. Tanner was biting rather than sipping the water.

"What are you doing? Is there something in the water you are trying to catch?" I inquired.

"T-t-the light. I-I-I'm trying t-t-to catch t-t-the light. I-I-I want t-t-to hold it i-i-in my m-m-mouth."

I turned to Sidekick, questioning why Tanner was trying to catch the light sparkling in the water. I thought she must have put him up to it.

"I told him there was a magnificent mirror deep inside him, and that he was doing a good job of learning to catch the light inside and reflect it outward."

How silly, I thought, when suddenly Tanner began coughing and speaking at the same time.

"L-l-look! Upstream. T-t-there's something on t-t-that log!"

Tanner was right. On a large log floating down the river was a petrified cat, heading for the rapids that were audible downstream. Quickly, I looked around for some way to help.

"What should we do, Sidekick?"

Sidekick remained silent as the log grounded on a sandbar. The cat was too frightened to move and still needed to find a way to cross the six feet of water between the temporary island and the shoreline.

"Hold on! We'll find a way to help you!" I yelled.

I quickly climbed a shoreline cedar and perilously slithered out on a branch overhanging the water. My weight lowered the thin branch to within four feet of the feline, but it was still a questionable challenge. The long-haired cat seemed to be Birman, not a typical feral variety.

"Try to jump and grab the branch while I hold it steady."

The part of the log to which the cat was clinging was bouncing in the current.

"Move closer to the end of the log and jump."

"And then what?" came a timid response. "That branch doesn't have much to grab."

The end of the branch was less than an inch in diameter, but it was strong, with lots of greenery on it.

"You don't need much. You have four feet and eighteen claws to snag the tender wood. Just try. I really don't know of any other way to help."

The end of the log was still in motion when the feline jumped from its highest bounce, just barely snagging the meat of the branch. The captured branch dipped the cat into the glacial waters before I could back off and shift my weight closer to the tree trunk. The icy dip spurred the now-wet cat up the branch and against my chest, where it nuzzled against my fur.

"Oh, thank you! Thank you! Thank you!" came soft words of gratitude.

We both made our way to the ground, where Tanner and Sidekick were waiting for us. I was surprised to learn that the feline who had tackled the awesome challenge was a female, and very attractive once dry. Under her fur, I could see she wore a blue harness that perfectly matched her eyes. Her face, ears, legs, and tail were dark. She had white paws with one dark spot on each right one, and a creamy tan torso.

As we settled in for the evening, I introduced each member of our clan, and asked the cat her name and how she came to be in a wild forest mountain stream.

"My humans call me Suki Lover, but I prefer just Suki. We stopped at a campground upstream, and my humans departed for a day hike. They left me behind in the tent, where I enjoyed a long nap. But I became restless in such a small space as the sun got warmer. I attacked the bottom junction of zippers on the front flap until I could squeeze my nose and, eventually, my entire body, through the opening. Pleased with my escape, I sauntered off in search of adventure.

"Unbeknown to me, however, in the next campsite was a rottweiler who considered me fair game. The chase took us through the length of the campground to the river's edge. My only escape from his jaws was to walk the length of a stranded log. Unfortunately, the weight of the dog at the opposite end loosened the log's mooring, and I started floating downstream. At first I was relieved to be out of sight of the dog, but then the log began to pitch and roll as the current became wilder. Once it even spun in a complete circle. Then I realized that a log, controlled by a raging current, was not a safe place to be."

"W-w-what an a-a-adventure!" exclaimed Tanner.

"Yes; not exactly what I had in mind for the day, but you know what they say. If you have no struggles, you must be asleep."

What a female! I thought. Suki was courageous, philosophical, humorous, and beautiful. She raised her back leg and continued licking the fur along her tan hipline. I decided to give her some privacy and wandered back to Tanner. He was also licking the few remaining hairs on his shoulder.

"S-s-she doesn't look much like you, Topper, but she's a nice addition to our family. I hope she knows she's welcome in our home."

I was delighted that Tanner considered us a family, content with our traveling home. He no longer thought himself an outcast. Those who met him made no mention of the stutter that he thought had previously distinguished him as different.

"She's unusual all right, but I saw others like her when I lived at the animal shelter. The breeders didn't want Birmans who didn't conform to the standard all-white-paw look, so they took those who were different to the shelter.

"By the way, Tanner, did I ever tell you that I knew another fawn with your name? Sidekick and I always thought Pretty Lady's son, Tanner, would grow up to be Prince of Ravenwood. Maybe you'll be a prince someday too."

"I wish I could have met him," stated Tanner solemnly. "A prince is noble, isn't he?"

"Hey, Tanner, you didn't stutter!" I said excitedly, but Tanner didn't respond. He was curled up, sleeping peacefully. I took my place next to him and was lulled into sleep by the rhythm of his heart.

Long before dawn, I woke suddenly to a lugubrious cry that startled me, but by what? I looked around to see what had changed. Sidekick was nestled under a cedar, Raven was on his perch, and Suki was curled in a patch of ferns. I hadn't been dreaming, nor had I been struggling with any problems. The events of the previous day had been exciting, but I wasn't restless from them. A breeze moved over us like a wave and stirred shadows in the night.

The sky was full of stars, my nose was frost stung, and my bones were shaking from some irrational horror, an internal earthquake for which I had no explanation. Shafts of moonlight and starlight filtered through the trees on this tranquil night. Silence indicated that the night life felt no threat to their territory. I snuggled close to Tanner's cold, hairless body. All was quiet around me. Too quiet.

I took a quick bath and stretched slowly into a curved repose. Suddenly, a storm of emotion chafed my insides. With a shuddered breath that sent chills down my spine, I realized the heartbeat that had lulled me to sleep had stopped. Prince Tanner was dead!

Here and Now, Together

T ears descended uncontrollably from my burning eyes. It didn't make
    sense that the force that had created Tanner would have destroyed
its own idea so early in life. Sidekick and Suki were still sleeping. In the
darkness, I reviewed the moments that I had shared with Tanner. He
was kind, anxious to please, and willing to demonstrate everything he
learned. He had been physically weak from the day I met him, but to
the end, he was philosophically strong.

A prince is noble were the last words he uttered, and noble he was.
Tanner belonged to a class of animals who demonstrate high values
and fine qualities. He was born that way, but unlike some animals who
lose their innocence during challenges, Tanner never wavered. In that
respect he *was* different, and a welcomed addition to my life.

There was little comfort in anything Sidekick or Suki said when
they woke to the sad news.

"He was proof to the world that happiness resides inside you," stated Sidekick. A single tear appeared to drop from each of her large brown eyes.

"I'm so sorry," Suki consoled me. "I didn't know Tanner, but I can see how much he meant to you. When you're ready, please tell me all about him. He must have been very special to be your friend."

Suki licked the side of my face and paced back and forth, her body and tail slithering under my chin.

"He was a friend to the world," I sobbed. "You would have liked him too."

I walked once more around Tanner where he rested amid a profusion of plants, and thanked him again for being someone special in my life.

"He chose a good place to rest, until it comes ..." I hesitated.

"Tilitcomes? Is that the name of this place?" queried Suki.

"Errr, yes," I finished. "Tilitcomes is the name of Tanner's new home."

Sidekick gave me a smile as she turned to head down the trail. She knew why I had stopped in midsentence. I didn't want to leave the image in Suki's young mind of what would inevitably happen to Tanner. Tanner would rest peacefully for a short while, until it came time for him to give the body he no longer needed back to the earth. In time, the calcium in his bones would provide nutrients for the trees and other animals.

As we crested each hill later in the morning, I paused at its apex to sorrowfully look back toward Tilitcomes, now shrouded in a misty aura.

"It's time for you to learn about here and now," announced Sidekick. "Remember yesterday when Suki traveled fifty yards down the river without moving her feet? While she clung to the log, it transported her effortlessly from there to here, from then to now, through the rapids into calm water. Life is an endless river of here-and-now episodes. As we pass along, we encounter various experiences, but we are always in the present moment. Those experiences are all a part of the here and now.

"What happened yesterday isn't in the past; it's in the present, as long as you live its lessons. Likewise, what will happen tomorrow is already occurring if you are preparing for it today. Therefore, all that really exists is forever held in the present moment."

"Wow, Sidekick! Do you really expect me to understand that?"

"Eventually. If you ponder it, this concept might help relieve some of your sorrow."

"Will this sadness ever go away?" I asked hopefully.

"Maybe not completely, but eventually your sorrow will turn to joy again. Right now you are in the center of an emotional storm. Even though it's painful here, this is the best place to find answers because you're ready to get out."

"Kittens!" exclaimed Suki. "Ah, look, they're all alone."

Before Sidekick or I could respond, Suki had joined a pile of mewing kits tucked behind a brush pile at the opening of a hollow log.

"Be careful, Suki," I warned. "Those aren't domestic kittens; they're bobcat kittens. The mother is never beyond their sound."

I watched as Suki affectionately bathed the face of each kit and calmed its crying. *What a wonderful mother she would make*, I thought as I recalled the love with which my mother had bathed me. Suki's gentle instinct was natural material for motherhood.

"We can go now," replied Suki. "I just wanted to comfort them. I'm sure their mother won't mind."

As we walked along, Suki described for me her life with humans. She had lived with an adult man and one child named Tess. According to Suki, the man had adopted her from a shelter to provide company for the child.

"Tess is also different," explained Suki. "Two years ago she had an accident that injured her leg and changed her enjoyment of life."

"Gosh, injuries can be terrible!" I responded.

"She isn't totally incapacitated, but some days it is painful for her to walk around. Knowing I didn't understand how serious an injury Tess had suffered, Suki continued to explain after pausing to remove a burr from her front paw.

"Her father leaves her with me when she gets upset to the point of crabbiness. I try to calm her, but you can't imagine how much purring is required sometimes before she is able to enjoy a long nap."

"I hope you will decide to stay with us a long time, Suki. We could have great fun together."

"Oh, I can't stay, Topper. I have to get back to Tess. She needs me. I give purpose to her life. Without me, she would have no one to talk to, or feed, or stroke. I matter to her and she matters to me."

I couldn't fault Suki's reason, because I had loved my human, Maggie, and was saddened when she left.

"How do you plan to find your humans, Suki?"

"I've learned never to plan anything, Topper. I'm just going to follow the river. My humans play on the river every weekend in summer. Sometimes they camp. Sometimes they kayak. I'm sure we'll find each other soon."

For Tess's sake, I hoped Suki was right. I enjoyed the sound of Suki's loud purr as it lulled me to sleep. The rhythm of her heartbeat had a calming influence on me when my thoughts were troubled. Everything about her gentle nature exuded loving kindness. I understood why Tess would need someone like Suki in her life.

While we were talking, we passed Sidekick at a walk. Her gait was very slow, allowing dust to eddy around her feet as she dragged them along. None of us had eaten much on this journey, but somehow Sidekick's belly seemed larger. Her emotions seemed a bit shaded too.

"Coming through!" shouted Raven as he plummeted thirty feet to snare a snake in front of us. "Excuse me while I wrestle with this creature."

With one foot, he pinned the tail of the snake to the ground. He used his beak to squeeze the middle of its long, narrow body. The snake opened its mouth as wide as possible and turned to strike Raven on the neck. Just as quickly, Raven tossed the reptile over his right shoulder and lunged at it again, pecking hard to tear the tough skin. Not wanting to observe the inevitable demise of the snake that would become lunch for Raven, Suki and I moved on past a row of hemlocks that followed a line of decomposed cedars.

We were entering an area of shadow-laden river canyons. The sound of falling water inundated our ears. Here, the river behaved like the mountain wind, constantly forcing its way around obstacles without pausing or retracing its path. An area of unclaimed treasure, Sidekick called it.

"I'm sorry to be so slow, Topper, but I must rest again," groaned Sidekick.

"Can I get you anything?" I asked as I noticed her struggle to the ground.

"No, thank you. You and Suki enjoy yourselves while I rest. I won't delay us long."

Suki and I decided to play a game of chase through the ferns. Tumbling all around, we dusted ourselves in their fine pollen, occasionally sneezing to clear our sinuses. I made a final lunge at Suki, knocking her into a pile of bramble.

"Hey, take it easy!" she shouted as she rolled to her feet. "Ouch! Let go!"

"I'm not holding you."

"Well, something is, and it won't turn me loose."

I walked around Suki as she twisted, yanked, and tried to pull her body through the harness that was restricting her.

"I'm caught … on something … prickly!" she protested impatiently.

"Hold on, I'll get you loose," I assured her.

Suki's last roll on the ground had landed her in a prickly patch of blackberry vines, which managed to secure an unbreakable grip on the back of her harness. No amount of pulling would untangle the mess that was only holding her tighter with each wiggle.

"I'm going to chew the part of your harness that's around your neck, and then maybe you can slip out."

"Well, get to it. This thing is choking me. Hurry up, Topper, I don't like being confined."

I had never seen Suki so agitated. She suddenly lost all patience.

"Oh, my gosh, Topper, chew faster, chew faster. There's something coming."

Before I could turn around, I heard the snarl of a hungry coyote advancing behind me.

"No! Go away!" I shouted, but it didn't obey.

I stood in defense of Suki against a determined adversary. The coyote was drooling and its clearly protruding rib cage left little hope we could change its course for dinner. Suki was frantically twisting behind me as I made myself as large a target as possible. This wasn't a situation from which I could run or out-finesse the predator. I had to stay and fight until Suki got loose. I wasn't afraid to fight in defense of someone I loved, but I was afraid I couldn't fight long enough for Suki to seek the safety of a tree. I had time for only one deep breath before the battle ensued.

In a single bound, the coyote pinned me to the ground, where we wrestled in the dirt. It snarled as I hissed, spat, and shrieked at its attempt to shake me senseless. Briefly, I panicked; then I scratched ferociously at its eyes and throat. My eyes were closed now as I simply responded to my own pain with unretracted claws. I would hold on as long as I could, hoping that it would be long enough. I didn't need to measure the progress of my battle visually. All I needed was time, and Raven.

"Raven!"

My call was loud, and immediately Raven responded with an aerial attack, distracting the coyote so that I could escape to chew loose the last bit of Suki's harness and help her slip free. Sidekick heard the commotion, and joined Raven in convincing the predator to retreat.

The battle was over, but my pain was just beginning. With the rush of adrenaline gone, I began feeling weak from the bruises and cuts to my body, inflicted by the unfortunate and vanquished coyote.

"Oh, Topper, Topper, you're wonderful and courageous! The most excellent cat I've ever known!" Suki praised me. "Thank you for defending me against that coyote. I'll never forget what you did."

Suddenly, receiving all of her praise and appreciation, I didn't want to be anywhere else anymore. I wasn't in a hurry to find Matie or a new home. The pain was replaced by contentment, and I couldn't imagine any place better than Suki's shoulder.

My heart had spoken to me. Now, how could I tell Suki how I felt? I wanted to share with her all of my thoughts and feelings. I wanted to know about her experiences. Most of all, I wanted her to know that she was special in my life. Her presence gave my life new meaning.

My heart was beating rapidly with excitement when Sidekick interrupted and suggested that we leave. As long as Suki joined us, I would go anywhere.

"This area is treacherous," advised Sidekick. "Until we reach a lower meadow where the river flattens out, be cautious!"

As Sidekick took the lead, I noticed that her stance was wider than usual. There was something about her gait that didn't seem normal. Observing her hoof prints, I noticed that her hind feet didn't overlap the front prints. They were farther apart in width, which explained her slight waddle.

Suki, on the other hand, had a graceful gait and a cute wiggle when she trotted. I loved the way her tail flirted as she bounded over obstacles. Following her was sheer joy and I felt no impulse to lead the way. How fortunate we were to have met! Had the fire not driven us out of Ravenwood, I would have met neither Tanner nor Suki. I hoped that all of our other friends had escaped the fire and were safe with new acquaintances, new homes.

"Tell me about your home, Suki. Where is it located?"

"We live on the outskirts of town, where the river meets the sea. My humans raise milk cows and grow vegetables for sale in town. The man knows all about different animals. Tess and I watch him tend to sick cows, and neighbors horses too. But most days are uneventful." She panted as she changed her gait to a gallop. "Tess and I usually stay close to home. In summer, I chase flies while she rests in the hammock. In winter, I bathe and nap while she reads to me. Wherever she goes, I go too."

Suki's voice had a tinge of urgency in it. I could tell that thoughts of Tess troubled her. How was Tess going to manage without her? How would I manage without Suki? I didn't want to consider that possibility. I was simply grateful for every day we spent together.

"Tess and I really didn't like the summer camping expeditions," Suki continued. "We preferred the comfort of our home routine. Her father liked the quiet of the forest and the night sounds, but Tess couldn't fully enjoy the wilderness trips from her camp chair. Her inability to move about freely frustrated her to the point of tears, so I always had more difficulty comforting her when we camped. I had to purr loudly all night to keep her calm."

"That must have been hard on you."

"Well, it's why I didn't say much to you when we first met. My throat was still rather sore from purring the night before."

"I wondered why you didn't scream for help from the log. I just thought you were being brave."

"Actually, I didn't think there was much chance of anybody rescuing me even if I did yell. I didn't think there would be two crazy cats in this forest!" joked Suki.

Flagging her tail, Suki batted me with her paw and ran ahead.

"What a cat!" I sighed and followed her obliviously.

Sidekick stopped along the river for a drink, and we joined her.

"It's amazing, isn't it, Topper?" commented Sidekick. "The river is as old as the mountains, but each sip we take is from new water. A drop only passes this way once."

I didn't know how to reply, but I knew there must be a lesson in her statement somewhere. The sun sparkling on the water reminded me of the day Tanner tried to catch the light in his mouth.

Be a mirror for the light, and reflect its beauty, Sidekick had told him. It was the lesson Tanner learned the day we met Suki. At the time, I thought it was silly, but now I contemplated its meaning for myself. Tanner didn't let the kindness he was shown stop with him. He magnified and reflected it. The compassion he showed others was greater than that which he received. Although Tanner's life had been brief, it was surely happier than Rat's.

A cool breeze from the mountains ruffled my fur. By now, the brilliant colors of the mountain flowers were absorbing the heat of the sun, trapping it in their hairy leaves. Delicate spring snowflakes, melted by the spring warmth, now filled the glacial streams that irrigated the lowlands and, like us, passed this way only once.

"These darn burrs are everywhere!" complained Suki. She spat out a mouthful of hair along with a few burrs.

"Let me help," I offered. I showed her how to pull the burr gently between her teeth along the length of the shaft of hair. "Isn't that better? This way you eliminate the burr without losing so much fur."

"I suppose, but I'd rather avoid them altogether if I could see them in advance. They seem to spring up only as my tail passes by. Stealthy little plants they are."

"Quiet!" whispered Sidekick, with tail and ears at full alert. "Something is moving through the ferns."

Momentarily, we all remained still. The noise and movement were coming toward us now, and whatever it was, was large.

"This way, Suki," I directed. I leaped across her back and headed up a tree. She followed with her nose on my tail. Sidekick bolted in the opposite direction.

"Hey, who's there?" called a familiar voice, tentatively, in response to our movement.

Sidekick stopped in her tracks and turned around.

"Matie? Is it you? Oh, Matie, I'm so glad we followed the same trail!" exclaimed Sidekick with an energetic display as we came face-to-face with Matie.

"Oh, Sidekick! Me too. I kept watch behind us, but nobody from Ravenwood ever came. What took you so long? Where's Topper? Did he come with you?"

"Here I am!" I announced and vaulted down the tree. "I have someone I want you to meet. Her name is Suki. She's, eh, well, eh, a good friend."

"So nice to meet you, Suki. Were you escaping the fire too?"

"Not the fire," explained Suki as she gave Matie's front leg a head-to-tail rub. "Topper helped me escape the river."

"Sounds like you've had an eventful journey, Sidekick. No wonder you were so far behind me. Have you seen anyone else?"

"Just Raven. He's been leading the way. He's flown ahead to scout tomorrow's territory. How about you? Did you have trouble making it all alone?"

"Well," began Matie, "I wasn't exactly alone. It's okay, you two! You can come out now."

Hidden behind the ferns were Matie's twins. They cautiously made their way forward.

"What perfect fawns!" Sidekick complimented her. "They have your nose and ears."

"And my appetite!" Matie laughed. "They're a bit small, but that's because they arrived early. My fearful flight scared them out of me a few weeks before they were due. I'm afraid it might have affected Igo, because he and Lia are exact opposites. She's patient and obedient, but Igo has his own mind and, I'm afraid, bad intentions. I don't know how two fawns from the same womb can be so different."

"He's just a different kind of challenge, Matie. Nothing you can't handle," Sidekick assured her.

"Maybe, but the other day he hid from me and didn't respond when I called. We were descending the steep cliff by the waterfall when he jumped me from behind and nearly knocked me down the embankment. I've never had a fawn like him."

"We're all here to help now, Matie," I offered. "Suki and I will keep an eye on him." I probably should have conferred with Suki first, but she was playing chase with Lia, and I didn't think she would mind the job.

"Speaking of Suki," hummed Matie, "what a beauty she is! Do you two have eyes for each other?"

"Oh, stop it, Matie," I responded in embarrassment. "She's a beauty all right, but she belongs to a little girl named Tess. Someday she'll have to return."

"Uh-huh," came her mocking reply.

I was glad that at last we had caught up with Matie and the twins. Of all the animals from Ravenwood, I was delighted that Matie had chosen the same direction for her search. I knew Matie's previous offspring and was impressed with how well she had monitored and corrected their behavior. She was a kind but firm disciplinarian, always making sure the fawns' behavior didn't offend anyone else. Igo seemed a strange name choice, but perhaps it had something to do with his behavior.

Along the path, we told Matie all about our journey. Sidekick described my wet river crossing. I told about how we met our noble prince Tanner, the sneaky Rat, and Suki's adventure on the log. As we watched and talked, Lia and Igo pranced around the group, darting one way and bounding another while Suki followed.

"It's such a relief to have the security of friends once again." Matie sighed. "Shared responsibility is so much easier than raising them all alone. Igo never wants to nurse at the same time as Lia. I have to continually interrupt her meal in order to chase him through the forest. Poor thing, she never complains."

"Does Igo nurse when he returns?" I inquired

Matie thought for a moment and replied, "Yes, he does. As a matter of fact, he gets a rather long drink because I'm usually too tired from chasing him to object."

I nodded understandingly but said nothing. It was clear to me that Igo had developed a cunning way of receiving more than his share of milk, and as long as neither his mother nor sister caught on, he would continue his antics. Not sure how to proceed, I discussed the matter with Sidekick when we were alone.

"You were wise not to say anything to Matie just yet," advised Sidekick. "Mothers don't like to be told how to raise their fawns. It's better if you correct the fawn when he misbehaves. As a member of the community, you have that right. Teaching the fawns is a community effort and responsibility."

"But how can Matie be so blind to Igo's intentions? If she saw these traits in others, she would put a stop to them."

"A mother's love for her son trumps everything else. Her deep emotions weigh heavily in his favor. She doesn't want to believe of him what is obvious to her, so she keeps giving him another chance."

"Well, it doesn't seem fair to Matie, Lia, or Igo to allow him to continue this manipulation."

"That's where the community helps. We aren't as emotionally involved with Igo. We can be quick to respond when he is late arriving or doesn't follow through on what he says. We can tell him that his actions indicate he is thinking too highly of himself and too little of others. A single mother has to choose where she puts her effort. With so many worries bogging down her mind, it's difficult for her to deal with all challenges equally. She has to find a nice home, an ample food supply, safe play areas, and suitable companions. Additionally, she must respond to the unpredictable daily concerns for her family. That is a lot for any animal!"

As a male cat, I had never had sole responsibility for raising youngsters, but I could remember the difficulty my mother had keeping up with my siblings. Igo wasn't so different from my sister Tanara. She would meow, climb the cage door, and dump the water bowl until an animal shelter caregiver arrived to hold her. Her tactics were different, but the result was the same. Like Tanara, Igo got what he wanted.

When Suki returned from entertaining Lia, I asked her if she wanted to have kittens.

"Sure," she replied, "but not until I learn much more than I know now. There's nothing easy about a mother's job. Kittens are all different. No one method or approach to raising them works for all. Some need special handling."

"How would you handle a kitten like Igo?"

"I won't know until I'm its mother. Until then, everything is only speculation. Mothers feel. Others speculate!"

Suki sounded like Sidekick. *Was this knowledge an innate female thing,* I wondered?

"Males have feelings too," I added.

"I'm not saying they don't. I am saying the actions of mothers are based on strong, primitive instincts as well as thoughtful considerations. I can plan many of my thoughts in advance, you know, like theories on raising kittens. But until I actually deliver them and lick their faces, I have no emotional element to add to the equation. As you know, changing the formula changes the outcome."

There was no point in pursuing this discussion as Suki had obviously thought more deeply about kitten-raising than had I. As we settled in for the night, a slight mist, hardly more than cloud sweat, dampened our coats in the polished darkness. Suki and I snuggled together and covered our faces with crossed paws.

New Lessons

The advent of summer each year changed the world. The pace of rodents slowed, to my delight, making breakfast an easy catch. There were enough voles aerating the soil to satisfy a hundred cats. Each female vole reproduced eight more voles every three weeks, so there was an ample supply for us, as well as for every hawk, eagle, and owl in the territory, while still ensuring the survival of the vole colonies. Elk departed to the tender grasses of higher elevations, leaving the lowlands to the deer, who didn't mind browsing the dried earth.

In winter, small animals had to stay active to maintain body heat and often had to consume their weight in food each day simply to stay alive. Due to a limited food supply, resident mountain animals were usually few in number and small in stature. The cold climate required that survivors come equipped with short legs, small ears, round bodies, and thick coats to prevent much loss of heat.

Now, in summer, there was no need for thick winter coats. Suki and I spent hours every day cleaning and thinning the long hairs from our protective winter fur. When Matie's tongue was busy with Lia, Sidekick helped groom Igo, which provided her an opportunity for discussion.

"You know, Igo, I once insisted on having my own way," began Sidekick. "My mother and sibling were killed in the road because they waited for me to follow them."

"Why didn't they go ahead?" asked Igo.

"Because, when my mother called, I told her I was coming. She believed me and waited for me to join them."

"Why didn't you go?"

"I had planned to go, but I got distracted. I knew I could catch up eventually, so I told my mother what I thought she wanted to hear, not knowing how it would change her plans. I was having fun and didn't want her to bother me again with her demands. Little did I realize that the consequences of my lie would be suffered by her."

"Wow, that must have been gruesome!" snickered Igo devilishly.

"Gruesome? It was devastating! Life-altering! I hope you never experience anything like it."

Igo looked down at his hooves in disgust as Sidekick continued.

"We are each only one character in a huge plot, but the loss of one affects the entire community. We are intertwined, and as thinking, caring animals, we must strive for balance in our lives. No one animal is more significant than another. Each has an important role."

I looked at Igo, distracted by his shadow, and thought that Sidekick's lesson was lost on him. At some point he would have to learn the importance of balance in nature in order to survive. He would have to learn that his own desires could not come first. It was the basis of the rules that Sidekick had taught me in Ravenwood. The extinction of one animal species in the food chain could disrupt the strength of the entire chain. But Igo didn't care. He was busy admiring the shape of his shadow.

I knew that Sidekick was trying to teach Igo a valuable lesson, but instead of learning from it, I was afraid he might use the example of her onetime defiance to bolster his own poor behavior. Realizing that nobody was faultless seemed to give him more reason to be even more problematic.

As Sidekick walked toward me, she flushed a snake out of the brush. We looked at each other, and then watched the snake make a wild escape.

"The wisdom of a snake," she reminded me, "is to hide its purpose and presence. We disarm it by exposing its intent. Once exposed, its threat is thwarted and it retreats."

I knew that Sidekick's comment had less to do with the snake she had flushed than with Igo. By revealing his disguised nature, she was arming our defense.

The broad river valley we entered made traveling much easier. Suki and I spent more time pouncing at butterflies when we didn't have to watch our footing on the steep shale of valley slopes. During bath time, we watched as Igo fought with Lia over browsing areas.

"Hey!" objected Lia as Igo walked into her shadow. "You are eating in my area."

"What designates this as your area?" came Igo's quick retort.

"You know the rules, Igo. An animal's personal space is defined by its body and shadow."

"I'll let you eat in my area if you wash my ears," bargained Igo.

"I would have washed your ears anyway when I finished lunch," replied Lia.

"I don't want to wait. Do it now."

Today is a day when only a mother could love Igo, I thought to myself.

"I'm worried about Igo," expressed Suki with great concern. "He's so demanding and competitive. He puts a bounty on everything."

"The fawn definitely has problems, but why does the bounty bother you more than anything else?" I inquired.

"Because it means he values nothing. He doesn't appreciate having a sister who is willing to clean his ears without an exchange program. He takes whatever anyone gives him for granted, as though his greatness is owed their benevolence. Sometimes he takes a thing before it can be given to him."

I knew what Suki meant. I had seen Igo leap in front of his mother to eat a patch of wildflowers before she had a chance to offer them. Wildflowers were a delicacy to deer, and there was great significance in sharing them. There was nothing admirable in claiming them.

The wildflower sweetness in the air seemed to draw the attention of all animals. While Suki and I were resting, I was awakened by the sound of furious wings. Not far from my head, an aggressive bumblebee confronted a much larger hummingbird at the blossom of an early-blooming digitalis plant. Head-to-head, the body of each animal remained motionless, their wings a furious blur. Finally, the hummingbird backed away and departed in search of other nectar. Intelligent discretion, I surmised; not the outcome I had expected.

With few confrontations, we managed to travel a great distance through areas that were home to many other animals. Sidekick had said that what she disliked about some newcomers to Ravenwood was their disregard for those who already lived there and a tendency to change everything in their new home to resemble their old one. If they didn't like the way things were in Ravenwood, she questioned why they had moved there. As we did not want to make others feel challenged or offended, we expressed gratitude to the residents for allowing us to pass through their territories without incident. This was our policy, but obviously it was not adopted by Igo.

Warm days brought more floral blooms and the arrival of wild strawberries. As dusk approached, Igo wandered away from the group into a patch of berries, where a raccoon was feasting.

"You'd better come back," I warned. "Those berries are his."

"I'll be back in a minute," replied Igo. "I just want a taste."

Discovering that the berries were pleasant to eat, and not willing to share this juicy treat, Igo used his sharp hooves to scratch the back of the bewildered raccoon, sending him scurrying into the forest.

"That wasn't a wise move on your part."

"Ah, it was just a scared raccoon. To the brave go the spoils!" he gloated.

I knew it wouldn't be long before Igo learned the advantage of having a large family. There might be more mouths to feed, but there were also more claws for a calibrated defense. As I ran back to the group, seven raccoons of various sizes quickly surrounded Igo and started their attack. His screams echoed loudly from hill to hill. I was soon met by Matie and Lia. Even Raven joined us in stampeding the raccoons, sending them up the trees. Igo did not hesitate to flee immediately, passing Sidekick without a word as she arrived to offer an apology to the raccoons.

"I tried to warn him," I explained to Matie as we retreated. "He wouldn't listen."

"I'm sure you did, Topper. Let's hope he's learned the importance of sharing and waiting for an invitation. If not, he may not get by so cheaply next time."

Matie gave Igo a scolding for being inconsiderate and endangering all of us. After little consideration of what he had done, Igo finished licking his wounds and then followed behind us. Soon he was darting helter-skelter across the trail that Matie was forging. We traveled a distance safe from any repercussions from the raccoons before resting for the night. Sidekick and Matie found much to discuss, although none of it seemed to be about Igo. They positioned themselves on our perimeter, and were still talking when I fell asleep.

I awoke to Suki staring at me. Only a short stretch away, she was sitting up with her tail curled along her left side, her front paws tucked neatly under her breast.

"What's up?" I asked as I stretched my hindquarters and nuzzled her neck.

"They're gone, Topper, and they asked us not to follow."

Only then did I notice that Matie and Sidekick were missing from their perimeter spot of the night before.

"Where did they go? Why did they go?" I fired back.

"They didn't say, but they ordered us not to follow their trail."

"Are they coming back?"

"I suppose so. They said we should wait here."

I looked around. Lia and Igo were still asleep. I realized that Matie would have to return to nurse them. This was the second time Sidekick had left the group without giving a reason. I wished I had asked Tanner where she had gone the first time. At least I knew she wasn't alone.

It wasn't long before Lia and Igo stirred and also asked about their mother. Lia expressed genuine concern for Matie and Sidekick, but Igo, true to form, complained that his mother wasn't readily available to nurse him.

"Look, Igo, I know your mother. She's reliable, considerate, and obliging. Stop worrying about your breakfast."

"Then why isn't she here to feed me?"

"Because not everything in her world happens according to your self-centered agenda. She has others to consider also. Matie and Sidekick are old friends. They wouldn't leave without good reason."

"Well, leaving with Sidekick during breakfast doesn't speak very highly of her as a mother," snipped Igo.

"Maybe not in your mind, but returning to you speaks volumes about her devotion to an arrogant son."

Igo had no retort to my final statement. He didn't even move. He just stared blankly into space.

"Topper, listen!" exclaimed Suki.

I tuned my ears to distant sounds, hoping to hear the approach of the two deer. Instead, I heard the faint sound of human voices.

"Those voices are coming from the river!" shouted Suki as she made a dash in its direction. "It sounds like Tess."

As we approached the raging river, the voices became more distinct.

"It is Tess!" cried Suki gleefully. "I'd know her voice anywhere."

Across the river from us was a campsite with two humans and a kayak. The smell of smoked bacon permeated the air as the wind carried the flavors of breakfast our way.

"Tess! Tess!" yelled Suki frantically. "I'm over here, Tess. Can you see me? I'm across the river. Look over here!"

Suki and I paced along the river's edge to no avail. The roar of the river was too loud for a cat's voice to be heard, and its swirling water was too dangerous for us to cross.

"Stay here!" I shouted. "I'll be back with help soon."

I ran as fast as I could back to the tree where Raven was perched.

"Raven! Follow me quickly. I need you to cause a distraction. I need you to get the attention of some humans to show them where I am."

Raven followed obediently. Upon arriving at the river, he immediately understood the situation.

"Are you sure those are your humans, Suki?" he inquired.

"Absolutely. That's Tess sitting by the fire and rubbing her legs."

In one high leap, Raven took flight across the river. He glided silently toward the campsite and landed next to Tess, who, in astonishment, called for her father.

"Follow me! Follow me!" repeated Raven as he took flight back across the river to where we were waiting.

"Look, Daddy, it's Suki!" shouted Tess. "Suki found us. She came back. I see you, Suki! I see you!"

"Well, I'll be!" exclaimed her father. "I didn't think we'd ever see that cat again. I wonder how it survived in this wilderness."

"Go get her, Daddy. Please, go get her."

At his daughter's insistence, the father launched the kayak and started across the river.

"It's going to be a rough ride," I warned Suki as we watched the kayak toss and turn in the current. "You'd better stay low and find something to hang on to. Are you sure you want to go? You know we'd like to have you live with us."

The look in Suki's eyes was one I had never seen before. It absorbed me, delighted me, and then saddened me.

"You are the most wonderful cat I've ever known, Topper. I love you and your friends for rescuing me and keeping me safe on our journey. If I could have one wish, I would ask that we all find a way to live together somehow. But right now I must go to Tess. You always knew I would have to leave, didn't you?"

"Yes, I knew, but I'm just not ready for the parting. It's so sudden. I thought that we would have more time together."

"I know what you mean, Topper. It's been brief, but we have good memories."

"I'm going to miss you, Suki. I've gotten used to having you around."

"I'll miss you too, Topper."

I couldn't hold back my tears much longer. What I felt for Suki I had never felt before. Something in me was different. I didn't want to stop feeling its magic. I was simultaneously happy and sad.

"Saying good-bye is d-d-difficult," I stammered.

"Do you wish we had never met?" asked Suki hesitantly as the human called for her from the approaching kayak.

"No. I have no regrets about anything we shared, just what we may never get to share."

Suki turned her head in slow motion and licked my cheek. Then she licked me again and rubbed her head along the side of my neck.

"You are what I dreamed of, Topper. Thank you for making my dreams a reality."

With that, Suki jumped into the arms of the man and looked back over his shoulder.

"I love you, Topper." She smiled and winked as the kayak pulled away.

Suki's deep blue eyes were ever hopeful, as though they were anticipating something good. I listened to the sound of her voice reverberate as I contemplated my reply. Not wanting to overstate my feelings and seem foolish, I started to repeat her words. Would repetition seem trite to her? I didn't want to hold them back, so I yelled, using the full capacity of my lungs.

"I love you too, Suki! You are the stars of my nights and the sun of my days."

As difficult as it was to have her leave, I knew she would be returning to loving hands that would stroke and feed her. She would be with humans who loved her, and I would be with my family.

Raven and I turned at the river's edge after watching the kayak bearing Suki cross to the other side.

"A tough call, but I think she made the right decision," approved Raven on our way back to join the others. "The right choice isn't always the easy one to make. Did you see the joy in the little girl's eyes? Tess loves Suki too."

"I know," I replied reluctantly. "Our love is only deferred, not denied. There's still a chance that we'll meet again someday."

"Might be so, you never know," rhymed Raven on an ascent to the sky.

As I reached Lia and Igo, Matie was arriving from the opposite direction.

"Where's Sidekick?" I asked in a worried tone.

"She's okay, but she can't return right now."

"What's the matter with her? Take me to her."

"No, you can't go. Nobody can go to her."

"But she's all alone in the forest. It's not safe."

"I'm going back to her," Matie assured me. "I only came here to feed the fawns and to tell you why we left."

I was glad that I didn't have to ask why they left. After all, it might have been their private business. As I waited for Matie to continue her explanation, Igo assumed his position at her nursing station and started thumping Matie's belly hard with his forehead.

"Ouch, take it easy! Give the milk time to flow. Why do you always have to be so rough?" scolded Matie.

"You're late!" argued Igo. "Breakfast is getting stale."

"Well, if you don't like it, back off and let Lia have it."

As Lia and I both knew there wouldn't be much chance of Igo refusing what he wanted, we resolved to be patient with our agenda.

"As you may know, Topper, this journey has been hard on Sidekick," continued Matie.

I didn't like the sound of where Matie's statement was leading. Such beginnings seldom ended well.

"I know. I've been worried about her. Her gait has changed and she's been walking much slower. I thought maybe it was because she had gained some weight along the way."

"Well, in a way, you are right. She has gained weight that has slowed her pace and widened her rear stance. Don't you know why?"

"I don't know. There hasn't been much grain to fill her belly. Maybe the food supply on this side of the mountain is more nutritious."

Matie's laugh embarrassed me. What had I missed? Had something about Sidekick gone unnoticed by me? Suki hadn't mentioned noticing anything.

"Sidekick is pregnant, Topper. She's going to deliver very soon now."

"Pregnant? When did she get pregnant?"

"Last fall, silly, while you were on one of your adventures. Sidekick is going to have Young Buck's fawn."

I rather expected that Sidekick and Young Buck were fond of each other, but I hadn't made the connection. There hadn't been much time to think about such things since we left Ravenwood following the fire.

"Did Suki know Sidekick was pregnant?" I asked.

"I think she suspected, but she didn't say anything," replied Matie. "Suki just obeyed our requests. Sidekick wanted to tell you herself, Topper, but she was concerned that you might worry about her."

"Well, yes, I would have worried, but I could have handled it."

"She thought you were already busy handling other issues in your life. We talked about it last night as I prepared her for this new experience. This morning we located a perfect place for her delivery. She is secluded, well protected by ferns, and there are very few scents in the area."

"So that's why you didn't want us to follow. You didn't want us to contaminate the area with our scent."

"That's right. Sidekick told me she thought she was going to deliver several days ago when she left you the first time and Tanner followed her. As kind as he was, she didn't think he had enough stamina left to defend her if necessary. In her condition, she definitely wouldn't have been able to deliver and then defend both Tanner and the fawn. It's fortunate she could wait until now."

"That's just great. Did you hear that, Raven? Sidekick's going to have a fawn!" I said excitedly.

"I heard! I heard! A new member for the herd." Raven was obviously practicing his linguistics. He was a great mimic of sounds.

"I have to get back now, Topper. Please keep an eye on my fawns while I'm gone."

"Always! And tell Sidekick I'm anxious to see her and the fawn real soon."

"I'll tell her," came Matie's fading reply.

Anticipation is a time stopper. The minutes crawled by as I anxiously awaited Matie's return. Would Sidekick deliver a male or female fawn, or even twins? How long would we need to stay here until they would be able to travel? Would Sidekick need a special diet while nursing the fawn? I hoped Matie knew the answers. It was fortunate that we had caught up with Matie before Sidekick had to deliver. I wouldn't have known what to do or how to help in a birthing situation. I wondered what Matie could do once it started.

Legions of clouds crossed the sky, combining their shapes and forming new patterns. I enjoyed scratching my back on the grass, identifying cloud creatures as a method of passing time. Sometimes the cloud creatures loomed and other times they transformed too quickly to be identified. As I rolled back and forth on the ground, I could hear the crunching sound of hemlock cones beneath me. All seemed well with the world. Even Lia and Igo had settled down for a nap. I slipped into pleasant memories of Suki, the imagined rattle of her purr transporting me into another time.

"Wake up, Topper, wake up!" rang the alarm of Matie's voice. "Sidekick is having trouble. The fawn is in breech position and she can't get it turned around."

"Breech position, what's that?"

"It's coming out backward and it's stuck. It will tear her apart. They'll both die. Hurry, we have to do something!"

"What should we do? I thought these things happened naturally on their own."

"Usually they do, but sometimes there are complications."

"Then what?"

"I don't know. It's never happened to me."

Matie was as frantic as I. Neither of us knew what to do. I had no experience in anything like this. I thought through my past memories. No experience in Ravenwood seemed appropriate, so I thought back farther, to life in the shelter.

"Humans!" I exclaimed. "Maybe Suki's humans can help."

"I thought they left this morning."

"Maybe not. Maybe Suki's arrival changed their plans for the day. I have to go see. Stay with Sidekick. I'll try to lead the humans here. Be ready. Come on, Raven. I need your help again."

Once again we returned to the river, where Raven drew Tess's attention to my presence on the other side. Suki, in her arms, began fidgeting when she saw me. Somehow I had to get the humans to follow me back to Sidekick. Once there, maybe they would know what to do. I made such a spectacle of myself that I think even Suki was concerned.

"Look, Daddy, there's the cat that was with Suki."

"I believe you're right, Tess. It looks like he came back to join her. Can't say that I blame him. She's a fine cat."

"Oh, Daddy, can we take him home with us too? He could keep Suki company while I'm at the doctor's."

"I don't know, darling. Doubling the vet bills isn't exactly in our budget."

"I'll give up something, Daddy. I'll give up going to the pool and theater. Then we could afford him. Please go get him. He's Suki's friend."

"Okay, if it means that much to you. Keep a tight hold on Suki; I don't want to chase after her again."

Obediently, the man crossed the river in the kayak and pulled it onto shore. Cautiously, he approached and called for me to join him. It was all I could do not to oblige. If the situation had been different, I would have jumped into his arms, but Sidekick needed me. As much as I wanted to cross the river to be with Suki, I had to convince the man to follow me. I waited for him to arrive within arm's reach of me, then backed slowly away and waited. Again he advanced, and again I backed away.

"No," I said, trying to sound convincing, and continued to back away. "Follow me. Come with me."

"I don't think he wants to come to me, Tess," shouted her father.

"Oh, please, Daddy, keep trying."

The man obviously loved his daughter because he pursued me until Raven led us to where Sidekick was moaning on the ground.

"Well, what have we here?" commented the man. Sidekick remained still and let him examine her. "You're doing this all backward, Missy.

You remind me of my favorite milk cow. She often has trouble birthing. Get up and let's see if we can get that young one to turn."

Very gently the man assisted Sidekick to her feet. With one arm around her neck, he led her in a circle until her knees were too weak to continue.

"You've got a stubborn one inside you, Missy. I guess we'll have to try something different."

I paced as the man rolled up his sleeves and ran his fingers through his golden hair. He patted Sidekick's neck and stroked her belly.

"I hate to do this to you, but I can't think of any other way around it."

I didn't like what I heard. At the animal shelter, humans said the same thing right before they put an animal to sleep.

"He's giving up already," I told Raven. "I have to find a way to stop him from hurting Sidekick."

"Wait!" advised Sidekick. "I don't think he's the kind of man who would give up so easily. If he were, he never would have followed you this far."

"All right," I agreed. "I'll wait, but let me know if he hurts you."

To my astonishment, the man lowered himself to his knees and gently slid his hand beneath Sidekick's tail as she stood next to him.

"Don't worry, Missy; I've done this before with my milk cows. Maude always seems to need a bit of help giving birth."

He locked his elbow and pushed with a rocking motion. Then he walked her around again. No matter what the man did, Sidekick uttered no complaint.

"I think we can get it this time," said the man as he repeated the action. "That's it, Missy. Breathe and push. Breathe and push."

Sidekick was now lying on her side, nearly exhausted. With his second hand, the man stroked the length of Sidekick's back in slow, wave-like motions. Unlike Matie and me, the man was calm and reassuring. He gently pulled on the front hooves that were beginning to appear from under Sidekick's tail.

"You can do it, Missy. Nice and easy. There's no hurry. Just take your time. That's it. That's it. Here come the front legs and head. Keep pushing, Missy. It's almost here. That a girl! You're doing a great job."

After a long push, which left Sidekick panting, she delivered a slimy bundle into the hands of the man.

"Congratulations, Momma! You did it!" exclaimed the man. He gathered the fawn into his arms and stroked it until it started breathing.

"It's all up to you now, Missy," he said as he placed the fawn beside her. "Clean her up and love her, then love her more each day. Teach her respect; help her enjoy a good life. That's all the advice I can give you."

The man continued stroking Sidekick as she cleaned the fawn and disposed of the birthing remains.

"He's a good human, Topper." Sidekick sighed. "Suki will be safe with him. Thank you for bringing him to me. I knew you'd find a way to help."

"I'm so happy for you, Sidekick. Your fawn is beautiful, yet no bigger than a weed. Have you chosen a name?"

"Not yet, but soon. I think I'll rest now."

"Absolutely, you should."

As the man seemed in no hurry to return to the river, I also looked for a place to rest.

"Would you like to curl next to the fawn, Topper?" asked Sidekick.

"Are you sure it will be all right? I don't want to frighten her."

"She knows nothing about fear yet. She only knows trust."

"Gosh! Wouldn't it be great if she never had to learn about fear?"

"Fear begins with disappointment, Topper. An animal places its trust in something that isn't worthy of it; then it learns to expect less from everything else. It's a terrible habit. After a while, discouragement and fear replace hope and trust."

"Then I guess we each create our own fears by not putting our trust in reliable sources."

"Exactly, Topper. In the end, the only thing that matters is what you believe; what you *can* trust."

The heartbeat of the fawn was rapid, yet she slept peacefully, with a slight whistling snore, resting for her next adventure.

It seemed that no time had passed before the whoosh of Raven's wings as he landed on a perch above me stirred me to my feet. I saw Matie and her fawns grazing nearby while Sidekick prepared her fawn for a meal.

"Where's the man?" I implored. "I was going to go back to the river with him. Why did he leave without me?"

Matie walked over to comfort me and said, "He watched as you slept, curled against Sidekick and her fawn. I think he realized that you already had a family here and didn't need a new one."

"I have to find him. I have to tell Suki ..."

"They're gone, tomcat," stated Raven. "They broke camp and left."

"You saw them go?

"Yes. I followed him back to the river. I talked to Suki while the humans packed. I told her all about the new fawn and how helpful her human was."

"Did she understand why I couldn't get caught? Why I couldn't go with him?"

"Yes. She thought you were very clever! By the way, she said she'd see you in the starlight, whatever that means."

Starlight meant a lot. Suki was letting me know that she wouldn't forget me.

"I wish you could have given her a message from me."

"Listen, tomcat, there isn't anything that I could have told her that she doesn't already know. This isn't a flash fire that you two have started. You're in for a long burn, an enduring relationship, a continuing story."

I had never known Raven to be the least bit philosophical, or to be so eloquent either.

"Maybe you're right. The long burn certainly describes the sensation in my chest. Why does it hurt so much?"

"I don't know, tomcat. That's a question for Sidekick. Ask her."

I didn't have to repeat the question; Sidekick had been listening to our conversation.

"The burning sensation is your heart changing, Topper. It's creating a strong bond that will unify the two of you. It's the second lesson of love. Until now, you have only felt the love of your mother, siblings, Maggie, and Tanner. Your love of Suki is symbiotic. It fulfills a different type of mutual need."

"How many more lessons of love are there?"

"I don't know. There are an infinite number of ways to feel and express love, and each loving encounter compels us to believe and trust more until we understand that love is fulfillment. Love defines the moment."

"Even Rat and Igo need love?" I questioned reluctantly.

"Yes," replied Sidekick soothingly. "Everyone needs love, but not all realize it. Those whose lives have made them sick, sad, jealous, scornful, or bitter are the ones who need it most. You are lucky. You know how to love because your mother, Maggie, Raven, and I first loved you. Some animals spend a lifetime learning how to accept and reciprocate love."

Sidekick was right. I had always felt comforted by my family and friends, but I wasn't sure I knew how to comfort them as well as they comforted me.

I asked, "How do I know if I'm loving correctly?"

"When you can love without needing to possess or change the one you love, then you will know you've done what was needed. Sometimes just being there is enough, as it was when Tanner died. He felt your affection as you rested next to him. Your love comforted him and eased his journey."

River's End

R aven rejoined me as Sidekick prepared her fawn for breakfast.
"I think Sidekick's having a rough time of it right now," Raven
said. "She hasn't seen Young Buck since the fire and has no idea in which
direction he headed. Those two have been friends for years."

"By the way, Raven, how is your family?"

"The young ones are coming along fine. They should be strong
enough fliers to join us soon. My mate was able to escape the fire and
find a vacated nest across the river before laying her eggs. It's a long trip
for me to make every day to provide them with food and give her a short
break from nesting, but it's worth it. Thanks for asking."

"I have great respect for the way you look after your mate and family,
Raven. Hunting long hours each day to feed them, and flying great
distances to lead us to a new home must stretch you rather thin."

"Thanks for the compliment, Topper, but she's the good one. I never
have much to show for a day's effort except for what I carry back in my
mouth, but she's always appreciative. Yes, she is. Never complains about
the selection. Just grateful when I return."

A loud scream startled Raven into flight.

"I bet it's that fawn again! Igo has probably stirred up more trouble," Raven said angrily.

"It can't be Igo. I just saw Matie's family head off in the other direction."

A second scream impelled us to seek its source. Flying low and traveling as quietly as possible through the thick undergrowth, Raven and I soon witnessed a standoff between a cougar and two bobcats. Normally, this would have been a no-brainer. The bobcats would have backed down from the much larger cougar.

"These two cats must have a reason for not leaving," whispered Raven.

The two bobcats, which had been standing together, slowly moved apart, forcing the cougar to make a decision. The cougar studied each cat carefully and growled another warning. The bobcats remained determined.

"Watch this!" whispered Raven, as he moved onto a heavily foliated cedar branch.

So intent were they on each other, the bobcats and cougar did not notice Raven in the tree until he jumped up and down, wildly flapped his wings, and let loose a cry that mimicked the cougar's. Uncertain as to what animal lurked in the tree, the cougar fled to survive for another day. The astonished bobcats laughed and thanked Raven for his intervention.

"Way to go, Raven! You sounded just like the cougar."

"All of my practice finally paid off. Let's head back and tell Sidekick so she won't worry."

A single beam of sunlight highlighted the area where Sidekick and the fawn were standing. The little thing had no trouble hiding between Sidekick's legs. Light-colored spots formed parallel rows down its back, and a dark mark on its lower lip added a touch of distinction. The fawn had learned to maneuver on its wobbly legs very quickly.

"I think we'll be ready to continue our journey tomorrow," commented Sidekick. "Iya may have to take it slowly while she learns, but I don't think it's safe to stay here much longer."

"You named her Iya? How did you come up with her name?"

"Her name means 'mother,' and she will grow to be a good one."

"It's a pretty name, but how can you be certain she will live up to it?"

"She was born with all the qualities she needs to be successful. Our job is to help her develop and refine those qualities."

"Well, you can count me in. I think you're right about leaving soon, Sidekick. We seem to be in a territory already under challenge. Raven broke up a standoff between two bobcats and a cougar just now."

"They must have kits nearby."

"That's what we thought, so we didn't stay around to find out."

"Topper, which direction did the cougar go when he left the bobcats?"

"He headed back up the river. Why?"

"We should leave now before the wind changes and he catches our scent. He's going to be looking for easier prey this time to boost his ego. Three fawns would be easy hunting for him. Tell Matie we're leaving now."

Once we were all assembled, we began a long but more gradual descent down the last mountain until the alpine ridges were no longer in view behind us.

"What are you thinking?" I asked Sidekick when she paused to look back.

"I just realized that I will never see the elfin forests near the timberline again, nor hear the cry of a marmot. The fragile mountain flowers will not have to contend with me in future summers."

"Do you know anything about the area where we're headed, Sidekick? Is it the same place we went to during the drought?"

"I only know what Raven has told me from his scouting trips. He said there are more humans but fewer natural predators. He suggested that we find a remote, forested estuary near the ocean where there will be ample food and shelter for all of us."

Iya and Lia walked together, laughing every time one of them stumbled. Their personalities were well suited for each other, leaving Igo to entertain himself. Although smaller than his twin, he was much larger than Iya, and he never failed to remind her of that fact, making her the subject of his jokes. Listening to him reminded me of the taunting that I had endured from Ka-newk and Ba-soht the day I lost my tail.

"I wonder what it's going to take to change the direction of Igo's life," I commented to Sidekick. "He's so much like Ka-newk."

"Change requires desire," replied Sidekick. "He will have to need and want to change. Then he will have to find something better with which to replace his old behavior. Changing is like eating. Just because salmon berries might make you sick, you don't stop eating altogether. You substitute a different food to sustain you. Igo needs to find something to like about himself as a substitute."

"The rate he's going, change may be difficult. His qualities seem less desirable every day."

"Yes, but every day those undesirable traits reveal his weaknesses. The larger he pretends to be, the smaller he must really feel. He pretends to be what he feels he isn't. We need to help him feel what we want him to be."

"What you say makes sense, but I don't understand why he is so different from Lia. She's thoughtful, quiet, and unassuming. She finds ways to be helpful, like encouraging Iya."

"Igo is different because he was born second. He lives in the shadow of his sister. She is larger, and was the firstborn twin of their mother. Lia was the first one kissed and nurtured. His arrival interrupted their established relationship."

"But Matie obviously loves both of her fawns. I haven't seen anything that she has done to make him feel second best."

"It isn't so much what she does as what he perceives, and how he responds to it. Thinking that his mother loves Lia more, Igo tries to be like her, but fails. He always will, as long as he tries to be something he isn't. His failure breeds more contempt and more poor behavior. We have to help Igo love himself, to realize that it's not important that he's Matie's second-born twin, but that he's her first Igo."

Listening to Sidekick's explanation made me feel sorry for Igo. Suddenly, everything he did seemed to be explained by his feeling unloved. As long as he didn't like himself, he didn't believe anyone else could like him either. Consequently, he didn't know how to reciprocate affection. How elementary it seemed! Feeling a little bit of confidence and affection might solve the problems with his behavior.

For the next several days, I assigned Igo tasks that I knew he could accomplish. I asked him to be in charge of finding a berry patch large enough to share with all the deer. I asked that he locate a grove of cedars with branches dense enough to protect us from the night dew. I asked him to take charge of Iya and teach her how to jump. Finally, I asked him to walk with his mother at the end of the day and, when she became tired, to provide her with words of encouragement. The more he accomplished, the less he required my praise. Sidekick was right. As he felt success, he began to like himself, and he became more considerate of others.

On our last trail down the mountain, we arrived at a junction that provoked an argument between Matie and Raven. Waiting on a rise overlooking the ocean and two paths leading to similar areas below, we listened as Matie and Raven disagreed over which path to take.

"Really, Raven, I don't understand why you are so set on taking the path to the right that follows the river. The left path looks more suited to our needs. There's a forest for shelter and a large browsing area. What's so great about the right path?"

Raven tilted his head to one side and perused the sky above us before responding.

"I just think we would be happier if we took the path on the right."

"That's not a good enough reason. There must be something else. Sidekick, make him explain why he wants to go to the right."

Sidekick walked over to where she and Raven could exchange a few words in private and then she returned.

"I'm sorry, Matie, but I must agree with Raven. The path on the right leads to something that the left does not have."

"Well, what is it? What does it have that is so special?"

"I'm going to ask you to trust us, Matie. You will find out when the time is right. Raven has checked it out and is certain that, as a family, we would be happier there."

As Sidekick was the most trustworthy animal any of us knew, we all consented to follow Raven's advice.

The path to the right led us across a broad meadow of native grasses and wildflowers. Large patches of blackberries lined its perimeter. Not only was this a good area for the deer to browse, but it was also home to an ample supply of rodents for Raven and me. Beyond the large meadow was a forested hillside of cedars, alder, maple, and madrona that bordered the river where it met the sandy shoreline. A perfect shelter for all of us. In this tranquil setting, the motion of the swaying trees and grasses were synchronized, the rhythm of the sea set the pace for life. The buttress roots of cedars that had lost their footing in the clay cliffs lined the cliff at the ocean's edge. Amongst these buttresses the tides deposited anything too heavy to follow the receding waves. Wading in the low tide was a blue heron, patiently hunting a meal as it took slow strides through the shallow water. Overhead flew gulls and eagles. Offshore, the rocky fortress of small sea stacks, sculpted by the battering waves, stood majestically. A peaceful setting for a lazy day.

The fawns were easily entertained by the waves as the rest of us relaxed near a log on shore. They chased the receding waves and quickly bounded in retreat when the advancing waves chased them. Occasionally they tugged on a detached strand of kelp or examined a new ornament dumped by a wave. This day at the river's end was a new experience for us all.

"Heads up, Topper!" warned Raven.

I heard the cracking sound of something landing on the rock next to me. Before I could move, a glaucous gull landed on the large rock to retrieve the contents of the clam, which he had dropped from twenty feet above me.

"Sorry if I scared you, dude," came an apology. "I didn't realize you were near my clam cracker until I had already released the shell. I'll share this one with you if you promise not to tell the other gulls. Some days I crack twenty, only to lose most of them to the beggars."

"That's a generous offer. I'd like to taste clam if you don't mind. I promise to take only a small bite."

I had hardly finished my morsel when I saw a flock of gulls approaching the rock to steal the remaining bits.

"I'll take care of this. Just wait," I said, as I positioned myself to leap from behind the rock onto the three gulls who attempted a landing on the first pass.

"Take that! And that! And that!" I shouted. I sprang into the air and pounced, stirring them into surprised flight. "Stop stealing from my friend!"

"Way to go! Hey, dude, you could come in handy. Could I interest you in becoming my clamming buddy? It wouldn't take much time, just once a day when the tide is extremely low. I could gather the clams and drop them on the rock, where you could protect them while I finish the job. Then we could share the catch. It would save me time. I wouldn't have to fight with the others, and I'd enjoy your company. What do you say?"

"It sounds like a good deal to me, but I'd have to insist that you eat two-thirds, since you will be doing all the work."

"Terrific! I'll see you here tomorrow. By the way, my name is Toobig."

"My mother called me Topper, because I always climbed to the top of the cat pile to sleep. How did you get your name?"

"My mother thought my egg was too big to hatch. See you tomorrow."

"I'll be here."

"We will be here, won't we?" I asked Sidekick after this encounter.

"Yes, Topper. We will be staying in this general area now. This is the trial period to see if it is the right fit for us. If it has everything we need and our presence does no harm, we will stay. You're off to a good start. Toobig will be a valuable friend."

Fishing with Toobig proved to be a worthwhile adventure. He taught me how to identify various aquatic animals and where to expect to find each one.

"Follow me, Topper. Today I'm taking you to the estuary while we wait for the tide to go out. I have a couple of friends over there that I want you to meet."

"What kinds of birds live only in an estuary?" I asked excitedly.

"They aren't birds, Topper. They're river otters, and their names are Rowdy and Rascal. Sometimes they swim along the shoreline, but mostly they can be found near the estuary. You like fish, don't you?"

"Absolutely! It's one of my favorite meals, but it's difficult to catch outside of spawning season."

"That's where knowing Rowdy and Rascal can come in handy. There they are, resting on a log."

Toobig announced our arrival and the otters graciously welcomed us to their driftwood.

"I understand you're new to this area," began Rascal in a sweet voice. "Where was your home?"

"High in the mountains in a forest named Ravenwood. My friends and I lived there until the fire drove us out. It was a beautiful place in every season. We were all very sorry to leave."

"Can't imagine how tough that must have been," added Rowdy. "Rascal and I have lived in these waters all our lives. Managed to survive during good and bad fishing years. Can't imagine living anywhere else. Can you, Rascal?"

"No. There's a nice cove up the coastline, but I prefer this river."

"Topper's a fish eater like you," Toobig informed them. "I thought maybe you wouldn't mind helping him and his friend, Raven, get a start."

"We'd be glad to help. Just send Raven our way occasionally, and anytime we catch an extra fish, we'll have him take it back to share with you."

"That is kind of you to share your catch. I don't know how to repay you."

"Don't worry about that now," Rascal said. "Someday we may need you to help us through difficult times. As much as we try to take care of ourselves, we all need help sometime."

Toobig and I stayed to watch the otters push off from the log into the river flow and head out to sea. In deeper waters they floated, curled around as though they were dancing, wrapped in each other's tails. Bobbing and dunking each other, they played as they searched for their next meal.

"I can't fish with you tomorrow, Toobig, because I told Sidekick I'd go back to the meadow with her. She needs some sweet grass for Iya, so I'll be hunting rodents tomorrow."

"That's okay. There's a farmer near the meadow who sometimes dumps grain along the shore of his pond. I don't know why he does it, because it isn't stale or mildewed. I could fly along with you if you'd like and feast on the grain."

"I'm sure Sidekick would be pleased if you did. See you tomorrow."

"Make it bright and early. The grain attracts lots of animals, and I want to arrive early enough for easy pickin's."

When I returned home, I told Sidekick, Matie, and Raven about meeting the otters and their generous offer. Raven said he would fly over the estuary every few days to see if they had any extra fish. Matie and Sidekick were excited over the prospect of grain and agreed to make an early start of it.

"I think I've flown over that pond before," said Raven as he looked in Sidekick's direction. "There's a farmhouse nearby and two cows in the field. I always thought it looked like a safe place to visit."

That night, curled up next to Iya, I found sleeping difficult. I couldn't clear my thoughts of Suki. I wondered what she was doing and whether she ever thought of me. Her dark face and blue eyes were still vivid in my mind, and every memory of her pleased my aching heart. I repeatedly told myself that I had to stop thinking about her and live in the moment. When that didn't work, I told myself that I would not think about her for thirty breaths. When that was successful, I extended the time to sixty, and then a hundred breaths, hoping to eventually attain a number of breaths large enough to hyperventilate and fall asleep.

"Someday." I muttered, "someday I'll see her again."

I repositioned myself and noticed Sidekick looking at me.

"What's up, Sidekick?" She moved closer to me and whispered.

"I was enjoying the smile on your face as you tried to fall asleep."

"Oh, I was thinking about Suki and remembering all the fun times we shared."

"That's what I thought. Special memories carry with them special smiles, aftersmiles, that warm us on cold nights and comfort us through lonely moments." said Sidekick.

"Yes," I replied. "Aftersmiles of Suki do replace the emptiness that I feel inside."

Since meeting Suki, I had felt emotionally detached from the world around me. My every roaming thought was of my attraction to her. Those thoughts completely pulled me out of the orbit to which I had become accustomed while living in Ravenwood. Now, it was difficult to feel happy without her in my daily life.

"You have to keep your emotions moving forward," whispered Sidekick.

"How do you know what I'm thinking?" I asked in surprise.

"You're moaning instead of purring. Emotions are beneficial if you live them in the present. Otherwise, you can create a lot of emotional waste."

"How can loving someone be wasteful?" I asked in a doubtful manner.

Sidekick's reply came immediately. "Anything that consumes your thoughts and actions is detrimental. You are a cat with many fine qualities, and your approach to life has benefitted many who have met you. Your purpose is greater than meeting the needs of just one animal. Great love fuels more love, lighting the way for others to elevate their passions also."

I knew that Sidekick was teaching me how to handle my emotions, but I was still feeling the full strength of my affection for Suki. I knew this lesson would not be an easy one to learn.

Morning arrived quickly, and everyone seemed eager to begin. Toobig and Raven led the way, while Igo and I encouraged the other fawns to hurry.

"Thanks for your help," I said to Igo.

"Glad to do it," he replied. "I've never tasted grain before. I'm anxious to try it. Hustle along, Lia! There's a surprise waiting for you."

Igo's new confidence delighted me. Instead of being offensive, his comments were now encouraging. He had won the battle over discouragement, and in his struggle, his true identity was emerging pleasantly.

As we approached the edge of the meadow, Matie pulled me aside and licked my neck.

"Thank you, Topper, for the help you've given Igo. He's the kind of fawn I always knew he could be, but I didn't know how to help him realize it."

"I didn't either, Matie, until Sidekick talked to me about helping him to be aware of his potential. I'm glad the change worked for him."

We continued our journey across the meadow and saw a bull elk standing amid concentric ripples in the center of a pond, where he was obviously cooling off in the bright sunlight. He was not attended by his cows, but was on a solitary adventure. Shadows flying along the ground warned us of aerial surveyors as we looked for the grain.

"I don't see it, do you?" I asked Toobig.

"Not yet, but wait. Here she comes."

"Here who comes?"

"The farmer's daughter."

"Is she bringing the grain?"

"No, Topper; she's too small to carry so much grain."

"Then what's she doing here?"

"She sits on the old log and watches the animals feast. Hey, here comes the man with the grain bag."

From my position on a mound of rocks, I could barely see the form of a human sitting on the log, or another carrying something on his shoulder. As we made our way across the meadow, the grass became shorter and more of the pond was in sight.

"It looks like she's just going to sit there and not bother us," said Matie. She approached the girl and bobbed her head in an attempt to flush her. The fawns waited in the distance until Matie and Sidekick assured them that it was safe to proceed. Eventually, each one of us approached the girl, cautiously looking for any indication that she might bolt toward us.

As I approached, something about the girl seemed familiar. She slowly turned her head, remaining quiet as though concentrating on individual animal sounds. Across her lap was a blanket, and at her feet was a small bowl. Since the grain did not interest me, I decided to examine the contents of the bowl. Very slowly I crept in its direction. What I smelled also seemed familiar, so I crept closer. Moving my nose across the scent stream and opening my mouth to increase my exposure to it, I suddenly recognized, from my days with Maggie, the scent of a recently opened can of moist cat food.

"Daddy!" shouted the girl. "Come quickly! It's that cat!"

The sudden movement and her loud shout sent all animals fleeing in various directions. My heart was thumping as I retreated to the safety of a tree, where Raven joined me.

"So much for a peaceful breakfast. Was this all a trap?" I asked Raven, but he seemed incredibly calm.

"It's not a trap, Topper. It's the reason I insisted we take this path. Look again."

Now, more carefully, I examined the little girl who was holding a blanket in her arms. The man standing next to her also looked familiar.

"Could it possibly be?" I asked Raven. "Is that the man who helped Sidekick?"

"Yes, Topper, it is. And the little girl is Tess. I followed them here the morning they broke camp."

"Tess!" I shouted. "Then where's Su—"

Before I could finish her name, Suki heard my voice and jumped out of the blanket where Tess had been holding her.

"Topper, is that really you? Oh, I couldn't stop thinking about you. I can't believe you're here. How did you find me?"

Faster than I've ever moved before, I hurled myself down the tree and into the four white paws that I loved.

"Oh, Suki, it's so good to see you too. I didn't know you were here. Raven followed your truck from the campsite. He never told me he knew where you were, but he insisted we follow this trail. He said he was certain we would be happy here."

"How long have you been here? Why haven't I seen you until today?"

"We've been getting accustomed to our new surroundings. I've met some great friends, like Toobig over there who taught me how to clam, and Rowdy and Rascal. They offered me young salmon."

"Does that mean all of you are going to stay here near the ocean?"

"Yes. Sidekick said we could stay as long as this place meets our needs and we don't harm it. By the way, Suki, your human did a terrific job helping Sidekick. Come meet the fawn. Her name is Iya. It means she will be a good mother someday."

Being with Suki again was like never having been apart. Our conversation began where it left off. She was delighted to see everyone again, and to meet Iya and Toobig.

"Everything seems the same," observed Suki. "Except Igo. He certainly has changed for the better."

"Tess seems happier too," I replied. "You have a nice home here with these humans. I understand why you didn't want to leave them. As a matter of fact, most of the animals I've met here are very helpful and graciously welcomed us to this area."

"It's because they appreciate what they have here. They hope you will learn to appreciate it also."

"I'm glad the river brought our two families together, Suki."

"As am I, Topper!"

Ravenwood

The Fifth Season

More Lessons

H appy once again to be with Suki, I looked forward to the warm days ahead. She was the same beautiful, loving feline I had rescued weeks earlier, and my feelings for her had only grown stronger.

"How did you help Igo to become a more helpful member of the herd, Topper?" asked Suki.

"Oh, it wasn't difficult once I taught him to look inside himself for satisfaction and approval. As he started liking himself better, he had more time to empathize with others in the challenges they faced, and he actually enjoyed helping them. All in all, he learned to meet his own needs by enriching the lives of others."

"Well, however you did it, it was a much-needed improvement that benefitted everybody."

"Thanks, Suki. Your appreciation means a lot to me."

As Suki and I continued to talk about our lives and adventures, I realized that home was not simply a place like Ravenwood; it was a powerful emotion. Home was where I felt safe to be my best and express my honest feelings. With Suki, I was content with myself, and she further strengthened me to face new challenges in the world unknown.

Days turned into weeks, and the warm days of summer gave way to the cooler days of fall. Each season I marveled at my increased desire to spend more time alone with Suki, rather than with friends and family. The depth of my emotion was almost paralyzing.

"Hey, Suki!" I said one morning as I ran to greet her. "How about traveling to the shoreline to help me guard Toobig's catch? We can feast on clams when he's finished."

"Sorry, Topper, I can't go today. I told Tess I would look after some feral cats she found in the barn. Perhaps I can join you another time."

Oddly, I took her comment to be a rejection of me; I didn't know how to respond. Not wanting to seem too out of sorts by her refusal, I decided to hang around.

"That's okay. I'd rather watch you teach the kittens anyway."

"Great, Topper, but you must keep your distance and remain in the background. Feral cats can be quite wild and unpredictable. Too many strangers might frighten them."

I obediently followed Suki at a distance and entered the barn very cautiously. The oldest cat was a handsome male seal point Siamese with awesome muscle definition. I was instantly jealous of his appearance. Two kittens had shiny gray coats. The male kitten was a skinny short hair with a patch of white on his narrow chest. The female kitten was the same color gray, but was much larger and broader, with a beautiful long coat and enchanting amber eyes. The third kitten was a male black-and-gray tabby with a target on each side of his rib cage. He had a handsome face with an expression of innocence and curiosity. All three kittens were struggling to see which one could climb highest on the stacked bales of hay. As Suki approached the kittens with her warm welcome, they introduced themselves as Jesse, Jasmine, and Mandu.

The introductions seemed to be going well until Suki slowly approached the handsome tom, who instantly growled in descending scale for her to go away. Unfazed by his warning, Suki continued her gentle approach. This time the feral newcomer hissed at her and laid back his ears. Still, Suki continued to advance, stopping just shy of the reach of his extended paw.

"Hello. My name is Suki, and I want to welcome you to our barn. What is your name?"

There was no response from the intruder; he arched his back and retreated from the kittens as he continued to hiss and growl at Suki.

"Please, won't you tell me your name? I'm not going to leave, and so it would be much easier to address you if I knew your name."

The stubborn male spat at Suki and retreated farther. *How horrible of him to behave so rudely!* I thought.

"Surely a name isn't too much to ask of you in return for a place of shelter."

"Fine then," he grunted. "My name is Kwaad. Now go away."

"What a splendid name for such a handsome cat. I like it very much, but I've never heard that name. What does it mean?"

"Anger," came his abrupt reply. "Kwaad means anger!"

"My, don't you have beautiful blue eyes!"

This time there was no response from the intruder.

"You will find plenty of mice in the barn," remarked Suki. "Tess would rather you not hunt the chipmunks as she enjoys watching them scurry. In the morning, you will find a bowl of fresh milk near the door. The farmer always collects the first three squeezes from Mildred and Maude and saves them for me. You are welcome to drink from the bowl before I arrive if you wish."

"Arrive? Are you coming back?"

"Absolutely. We have much to learn about each other."

"I've nothing to tell you and I don't need to know anything about you. I prefer to keep to myself."

"Nonetheless, I will return tomorrow. Good-bye for now."

I followed Suki out of the barn and asked, "How much longer are you going to tolerate this conceited fool?"

"Until he is no longer starved for affection."

"Affection? He doesn't even know the meaning of the term."

"Oh, my, if you are correct, wouldn't that be sad?"

"Leave it to you, Suki, to always think about the feelings of others. How do you plan to educate him?"

"Oh, I never plan anything, Topper. I just am."

For several days, I observed Suki as she patiently shared her thoughts and feelings with Kwaad, while leaving herself vulnerable to his attack and predictable criticism. He didn't understand the gift she was offering him.

"May I comfort you?" she asked repeatedly.

"No. Go away," was his tedious reply.

"But I only want to help you clean your ears and a few spots under your chin that you've missed."

"How many times do I need to remind you I don't need your help? I've managed just fine without you."

"Indeed, I can see that you have. As you feel you have no needs, will you comfort me?"

In a coldhearted tone, Kwaad responded, "Comfort you? Whatever for? I don't do licks and nuzzles. I'm not a needy cat."

Suki retreated, unscathed by Kwaad's remarks. She returned to the kittens, who were wrestling with each other. After several rounds of cutthroat, Jesse took a bath and left Mandu to confront the much larger Jasmine, waiting patiently on her side for the next advance. As Mandu was half her size, he had to predetermine which part of Jasmine to attack. He slowly circled her twice, grabbed her belly, and received a head thumping from her hind legs. Instantly, he jumped back, shook his head a few times, circled once, and attacked Jasmine's chest, pinning her to the ground. Jasmine responded by biting Mandu's ears until he released her.

Now Mandu required a thorough ear- and face-washing while contemplating his next move. Again, he circled Jasmine. She flipped from side to side whenever he passed her back. Finally, as he went past her head for the third time, Mandu grabbed Jasmine around the neck. From there, he could avoid a counterattack from her hind legs and mouth. He was able to maintain this hold for only a few seconds as Jasmine twisted her head, rotated her body, and quickly reversed the hold, putting Mandu in a double headlock that ended the wrestling match.

Jasmine retired to the haystack where Jesse had finished his bath. She watched as Mandu strutted across the barn floor to the bowl of milk, attacking every out-of-place straw in his path. Getting pinned three times by a female had not damaged his self-esteem. Suki and I chuckled at his antics as we left the barn together.

"I think I'd better head to the ocean to help Toobig with his catch before the tide comes in."

"Good clamming, Topper. I'll miss you."

Pretending not to care too much, I nodded my head in her direction and scampered off.

111

"Topper, Topper, Topper," groaned Sidekick as I approached her. "Pretending that love is a game has only one outcome. Every player is a loser."

"I'm not playing games!"

"Don't try to fool me, Topper. I know how deeply you care for Suki. To pretend that you care less or more than you actually do is dishonest. No relationship can survive dishonesty for long."

I felt ashamed for having wasted an opportunity to tell Suki how much I enjoyed her presence. I was embarrassed to tell her how much I really felt for her. Sidekick had warned me once before about compromises.

"Sometimes," Sidekick had warned, "a situation is either black or white. In such an instance, no compromise for a gray area will be satisfactory to either party."

According to Sidekick's logic, either I loved Suki or I did not. There was no room for anything in between, and to deny a reality would be of no benefit to anyone. Getting along with Sidekick was always easy because there was never any shading in her emotions. Her feelings were usually obvious to observers, so they could respond to her honestly if they chose. To Sidekick, there were no pardonable deceptions.

"When asked to choose between loving someone or not, the better answer is always in favor of love," advised Sidekick. "Either love is present in your life, or it is not. When Suki asked Kwaad if she could lick and comfort him, and if he would comfort her, she was asking him to choose which qualities he wanted to accept and express in his life. Love or fear? Joy or sorrow? Companionship or solitary existence? Such opposites don't dwell together, Topper, so everyone must choose. Whatever your decision, it will govern every situation in your life. You must be a willing receptacle of the same qualities you wish to give, Topper, and vice versa."

I knew Sidekick was right as I stared down at my paws.

"Tell me what you see in your paws," requested Sidekick.

Obediently, I re-examined my paws and described for Sidekick the individual callused pads.

"Where do you see the calluses, Topper?"

"On my paws, of course."

"You are deceived. Look again."

I continued looking at my paws.

"Topper, darling," suggested Sidekick, "you need to get the obvious out of the way in order to see what lies beyond it. See the world through your heart, not just through your eyes."

I yearned for Suki's affection. I looked at my paws again and tried to learn from Sidekick how to comfort Suki better. These thoughts rolled through my mind as I headed toward the ocean to help Toobig with his morning clamming.

As we rested together and enjoyed clam dinners, I noticed the large, flat surface of Toobig's feet.

"Whatcha looking at?" Toobig laughed as he wiggled his feet. "Haven't you ever seen a pair of webbed paddles before?"

"Actually, I've never paid much attention to bird feet, but yours are quite different from Raven's."

"Mine are exceptional! They're capable of propelling me quickly through the water and, being located in the middle of my body, they also allow me decent control when I'm on land." Toobig moved in a running waddle along the sandy shore and hopped onto a large piece of driftwood.

"Interesting! I didn't realize the importance of the position of your legs."

"Gosh, dude! Location is everything. The legs of diving birds are located farther back on their body to minimize drag, and to help steer and propel them through the ocean depths."

I tried to visualize what Toobig was describing and agreed that the leg placement of diving birds seemed like a logical feature.

"It's an advantage in water, dude, but on land it makes locomotion difficult."

I laughed as Toobig imitated the awkwardness of loons on land.

"Each species is adapted with tools for its specific needs," explained Toobig. "Birds who spend most of their time flying have shorter legs, so they have less weight to transport."

Everything Toobig said made sense, but I had never taken notice nor considered the purpose of differences in various species of fowl. I should have been more attentive to details after Sidekick explained to Tanner that every being is different and specially adapted for a happy life someplace where its needs are met.

"Are there other differences, Toobig? I want to learn more. I want to understand why certain birds choose to live here."

"Well," replied Toobig thoughtfully as he enjoyed a long stretch of his wings and a few preening tugs, "seabirds have a different metabolism and respiratory rate than freshwater birds. Sea water is toxic to non-seabirds who don't have our special excretion glands."

Toobig's explanation helped me understand why I had not seen the inland lake birds at the ocean.

"Look just offshore near that small island, Topper. Those birds are murres and auklets. What do you notice about them?"

"Hmmmm. They seem to be cleaning their feathers a lot. They have very short, narrow wings; chunky bodies; and large heads and beaks. Their legs are located toward the rear of their bodies. I'd say they are diving birds."

"Absolutely, dude! You can usually find them nesting on offshore islands during breeding season."

"Why do they isolate themselves?"

Toobig leaned over and whispered in my ear, "Dude! Because they are partially naked during the molting season!"

"Naked? You mean they have no feathers at all?"

"Well," replied Toobig rather sheepishly, "they still have insulating feathers, but they lose all of their flight feathers at once and are grounded until the new ones develop."

"Whooo! That must be a scary time for them. Hey, what are those crazy black birds doing lined up on that log with their mouths and wings half-open? They look tipsy."

"Those are cormorants!" Toobig laughed. "Their feathers aren't completely waterproof, so they're sun-drying them."

"Are they drying their tongues too?" I asked rather hesitantly.

"No, dude. Their mouths are open because they can't breathe if they are closed."

"Why not? Can't they breathe through their nostrils?"

"They don't have any external nostrils. Pelicans have the same problem."

I paused and considered Toobig's explanation.

"Now what's bothering you, Topper?"

"It seems rather strange that a water bird, like that cormorant, would not have waterproof feathers. That's all."

"You'd think so, but that feature actually serves them well when diving. It helps them sink when they squeeze out the air beneath their outer feathers."

"Weird! How do they store air in their feathers?"

"Not in the feathers, just between the layers of feathers. You've really never examined a bird before, have you?"

"Not up close. Why?"

"Dude! You're a cat! I just assumed you had dissected a bird at least once in your life!"

"Oh, I see what you mean. I took birds off the menu after meeting Raven. Fish and rodents are easier to catch. What were you saying about air between the feathers?"

"The outer contour layer of feathers defines our shape and repels water." Toobig pulled his wings in tightly and struck a formidable pose.

"The down feathers that lie between and underneath our contour feathers trap air and insulate our bodies. That's why we preen so often. We aren't exactly cleaning our feathers, as you mentioned earlier. We do remove parasites and such, but more importantly, we are re-hooking the barbules that interlock our feathers and help insulate our bodies."

"Right! I've watched you preen. I have one more question that I hope isn't too personal."

"Ask away, dude."

"Why do you spend so much time poking at your—you know, your tail feathers?"

"Ahhh, that's where my uropygial gland is located. Watch!"

Toobig placed his beak near his tail feathers and rubbed until a fine oil lubricated the top and sides of it.

"Can you see the sheen, Topper? The natural oils condition the feathers as I preen. As long as the feathers are lubricated, they remain flexible and are less likely to break during awesomely fierce encounters, don't you know."

"Hmmmm, I guess I do the same sort of thing when I bathe. I keep my coat clean and fluffy to keep me warm. Does a strong wind or wave unhook the barbules the way it messes up my fur?"

"Absolutely! Hey, this winter I'll introduce you to the visiting flocks. You'd better head inland for now. The evening breeze in on its way. I'll be clamming near the tidal pools tomorrow if you want to join me."

"See you then, Toobig. I hope you get another good catch tomorrow!"

Before I rejoined Sidekick for the evening, I wandered back to the barn, where Suki was still working with the ferals. Watching the kittens play reminded me of how fun life had been at the shelter. To kittens, fear is just an unexplored moment with a yet undiscovered potential for fun. Jesse, Jasmine, and Mandu vaulted each other in a race around the barn, spending very little time on all fours. Jasmine discovered an empty grain sack into which she darted. She blindly plowed her way around the barn floor with her hindquarters in the air as the two young males scattered out of her bulldozing path. The adventure ended abruptly when Jasmine butted her head against a pitchfork leaning against the wall. As the tool fell from its upright stance, it took with it a pail of culled apples that pummeled the sack like giant hail. Before the last apple fell, all three kittens were panting heavily atop the stacks of hay again.

I laughed. Kwaad spat and scowled. Suki checked to see that the kittens were uninjured. Jesse and Jasmine decided on a post-adventure bath. Mandu chased the shadow of his tail around and around his body, through his legs, and into a forward roll that landed him on his back. He momentarily viewed the rest of us from his upside-down and backward position. No action seemed to embarrass him. He continued falling and flopping around after failed attempts at acrobatics when most cats would have retreated to a sudden bath emergency.

"You enjoy watching the kittens, don't you, Topper?" asked Suki while I escorted her back to the house.

"You know me, Suki. I always enjoy a good laugh and the kittens provide lots of them."

"Then you should spend more time with them each day. They need your influence."

"But they have you and Kwaad. I'd just be a distant uncle to them. Too many adults could spoil their fun."

"You saw how Kwaad responded to them today. Either he pretends not to have feelings for them, or he scoffs at what he considers to be their foolishness."

"I don't know what you expect me to do. After all, he's their father."

"Not according to his thinking. He said they belonged to Raba, a female he fancied after the kittens were born. She was killed by a coyote after they found shelter in the barn."

"Still, Suki, he's already the head of their clan. It wouldn't be right for me to challenge him."

"Right? Do you think it's right for him to rule them with fear and apathy? With him, they will become the adult version of what they experience as kittens. Is that the change you wish for Mandu?"

Suki knew just how to persuade me to her way of thinking. I had only known the kittens for a short time, but she was certain the compassion I felt for them was more than Kwaad was able to accept and express at this critical time in their lives. I couldn't imagine my own life without the love and support of my mother, Maggie, Sidekick, and friends. Such darkness wasn't something I would wish on anyone. I agreed to help the kittens explore the joys in life.

"Suki, dear, you know that, even if Kwaad has no strong feelings for the kittens, he will still put up a fight. Without them, he has no clan. Their obedience to his orders gives him authority over them. Do you have a strategy in mind?"

"I never plan, Topper. I just am. I welcome surprises."

I wished Suki well and headed back to my deer friends. Along the way I thought how astute Suki was. By never planning for the future, she was able to enjoy everything in the present without limiting future possibilities.

The following morning, Sidekick and Iya followed me to the tidal pools. We heard the river otters diving and slapping their arms and tails on the water's surface as they appeared and disappeared in the distant tide. Iya tried to mimic them by stomping around in the sandy water puddles.

"Be careful, dear," advised Sidekick. "There are living creatures hiding in the sand and pools, waiting for the tide to come in."

Iya immediately stopped her splashing and lowered her head to examine the contents of a tidal pool.

"Look! Look! Look!" she exclaimed. "I see things. Many things! Many shapes and colors!"

Toobig heard the excitement in Iya's voice and landed gracefully a few feet ahead of us.

"So, little darlin', I see you've come to explore the mysteries of my world. What do you think of them?"

"They're so tiny and so beautiful! What are they?"

Toobig led Iya to a larger tidal pool near a huge rock covered with barnacles, warning her not to rub against their cutting edges. As she observed each specimen, Toobig identified for Iya the aquatic fauna and flora that waited in the low-surf tidal pools. Sea urchins, anemones, ochre stars, clams (of course), crabs, mussels, and transparent jellyfish, all slowly moved around their small world. Kelp and surf grass remained dormant, draped over the exposed rocks, waiting for the rising tide.

"I had no idea so many living things were hidden beneath the sea," exclaimed Iya.

"There is no place where life does not exist, dear," remarked Sidekick. "On top of the highest mountain and in the depths of the darkest sea, life is constantly reproducing its miracle."

Iya rubbed against her mother's neck. Sidekick responded with a nuzzle. I thought how fortunate Iya was to have Sidekick as her mother, rather than a doe like Ka-newk. My thoughts wandered to what had happened to the cousin herd after the fire in Ravenwood, and whether our friends had survived. I also missed the companionship of Raven, whom I hadn't seen since his return to the river where his mate had nested after the fire. He was waiting to escort his family to the new home he had built in a tree near the shore. He would also be a good parent to his offspring.

So many thoughts of family convinced me that I should agree with Suki and offer to be available to the feral kittens if they needed inspiration or help. Nothing I had planned to do was more important. Like Suki, I would enjoy what each moment had to offer. I shook the sand from my fur and joined Sidekick and Iya on the trek home under a dimming sky.

Contract with Life

Kittens are born playful and kind, and remain that way until they are exposed to fear. Challenging the unknown can sometimes upset a kitten's perspective of the world, and it is difficult to reassure them once they have relinquished authority to fear.

Kwaad's negative influence over three young lives, as well as over his own, was very strong. As hard as I tried to persuade him to consider accepting a more affectionate approach to life, he continued to hold fast to his well-established beliefs. He never talked about his past, but an unpleasant experience in his early years must have caused a great emotional loss that imprisoned his future. He had somehow managed to survive the tragic event, but at considerable cost to his own happiness. So closely did he guard his emotions that the muscles in his face had tightened to the point where they could not release his pain. Giving up on him would be easy. Going away and leaving him to his solitary ways would be easy. Forgetting about him, and returning to the experiences that made my life happy, would be easy. But easy isn't living, according to Sidekick, because it isn't learning.

"Life is progression, not regression, Topper," Sidekick reminded me. "No matter how many times Kwaad refuses your assistance, you must continue to offer it. No matter how many times he tells you to go away, you must remain on task. No matter what he does with his life, you must keep your contract with life."

"My contract?" I questioned.

"Yes; your contract to live your life as fully and beneficially as possible. A contract doesn't simply bind individuals together in a mutual agreement. It commits each individual to fulfill his or her part of the agreement, regardless of the changed opinions of others."

"I'll keep trying, Sidekick, but my persistence seems to anger him more."

"Just remember that your contract is not with him. It is with yourself. Don't ever agree to be less than what you are."

As inspiring as Sidekick's words were, I knew the task would be challenging. Kwaad would not be a willing participant. And so I entered the barn in a grand style.

"Good morning, kittens! What fun shall we have today?"

Immediately all three balls of fluffy fur ran to my side and enthusiastically offered suggestions. As early morning is often an active time for mice, I suggested we start with a hunt and proceed from there.

"Do as you wish," growled Kwaad as he headed out the door. "I'm going to explore the fields beyond the barn for a spot where I won't be bothered by your antics."

The kittens and I were very successful in our mouse hunt. With winter approaching, mice were scurrying everywhere, filling their storehouses with seed and grain. Mandu made the first catch. He patiently stalked a mouse until it was exposed enough that it couldn't seek immediate safety. Not only did his sudden pounce terrify the mouse, but his quick success so surprised Mandu that he dropped the mouse when it screamed. As soon as the mouse hit the ground, it took off running at full speed, only to be encircled by three more pairs of hungry eyes. As we tightened the circle around the prey, Mandu batted the mouse toward each one of us. We returned it to him until the mouse was exhausted. After tossing it in the air and between his legs a few times, Mandu gently placed the motionless mouse in his mouth and carried it to a corner of the barn, where he alone consumed it.

In one game of cat and mouse, I saw the kittens demonstrate that the playful antics of their games were now developing into hunting and survival skills. I remembered my mother encouraging me and my siblings in games that we accepted as fun. Sitting back to wash, I recalled that I had seen the fawns and other young animals engage in seemingly pointless play, only to see those same actions transfer to skills for hunting, foraging, and protection.

Bath time followed each successful hunt, leaving only enough time for a few bouts of sparring before Tess and Suki joined us. While Suki and I conversed, Tess gently held each kitten and combed its fur until it shone like silk, free of dust.

"Will you walk to the shoreline with me?" asked Suki.

"Certainly!" I agreed. "It will be a nice respite from our active morning. Is there something on your mind?"

"Yes, but I haven't discovered what to do with it yet."

Our stroll to the shoreline at low tide was quiet; there was no conversation or roar of waves.

"Oh my!" exclaimed Suki. "There are hundreds of gulls floating on the undisturbed, shallow water!"

At first glance, the shoreline water appeared to be so full of gulls that there was no space between them.

"Look again! Look again!" came the repetition of a familiar voice. Landing with a gentle splat in the wet sand of the shoreline was Raven.

"Welcome back, Raven," I said and I hurried to greet him. "Is your family well?"

"Indeed, indeed, and it has grown by two since you last saw me."

"We're so happy for you, Raven," remarked Suki. "Is your family nearby?"

"Not right now. My mate has taken the boys for a fly-around to get acquainted with the area. You'll see them soon enough, I imagine."

While Suki and Raven exchanged stories, I continued to take another look at the gulls in the water. Once again my eyes had deceived me. A closer, more thoughtful look revealed that there were only half as many gulls in the water as I had thought.

"Look, Suki, half of the gulls are reflections!"

"But they all seemed so real!" replied Suki in astonishment.

"Yep, yep," commented Raven. "That's why it's always a good idea to look and think twice in new situations. Look, look. Think, think," repeated Raven as he took wing to rejoin his family. "See you later!"

Suki stumbled closer and gave a long sigh of satisfaction. "That's just the inspiration I needed today, Topper. I need to reevaluate my thoughts. Something is trying to fool me."

"What is it that needs reevaluating? What's on your mind?"

"Let me first think it through for myself; then I'll share it with you. It's time to return to the kittens. Tess has probably finished grooming them by now."

The trip back to the barn was as quiet as the walk to the shoreline. Since Suki was deep in thought, I contemplated how to entertain the kittens upon our return.

That night, winter arrived in the lowlands. River rocks were capped with snowy bonnets and the barren bigleaf maple trees, trimmed in white, were a stark contrast to the evergreens. Mice, squirrels, and other animals that had stockpiled food for the winter were seldom seen. There was a hush in the forest.

"Brrrr, it's cold this morning!" exclaimed Iya to her mother.

"Run around a bit, dear, and you'll warm up quickly," replied Sidekick.

I stretched my forequarters, then my hindquarters, then gave myself an overall shaking to fluff my coat. After a few turnarounds, I settled down again before my warm spot became cold. It was still early morning, so I could see no point in rushing the day. I observed the remnants of a snail near my head and recalled how its foot secreted a fluid to make a slippery trail on which it traveled. *How clever*, I thought, *for a snail to create its own path in life and take its home with it.* The sound of Suki's voice interrupted my contemplation and startled me to attention.

"Topper! Topper!" she called pleadingly. "Oh, Topper, Kwaad didn't return to the barn last night. The kittens and I are very worried about him. Please, we must search for him."

"Calm down, Suki. Perhaps he left for an early morning hunt."

"No, he didn't. There were no paw prints in the snow around the barn this morning. He's been out all night, and you know how dangerous that is for a young feline. We must take up the search for him."

"Suki's right, Topper," added Sidekick. "I'll round up Matie and Raven, and then we'll all look for Kwaad. We'll meet you at the barn and search from there."

Suki and I returned to the barn to calm the fears of the kittens and waited for the search team to arrive.

"You know, Suki, even if we do find Kwaad, he won't be grateful for our effort. He likes being on his own."

"That's only what he says because he feels safer when he's alone. One night in the woods might change his thinking if he gets into a predicament beyond his control."

"I'm just saying ..."

"I know what you think about Kwaad, Topper, but let the discourse end with you. Stop feeding his fear!"

"Feeding his fear? I've spent hours trying to talk him into accepting life in a more positive way, and he hasn't budged from his opinion."

"Then it's time to stop talking, time to start living what you believe," advised Sidekick as she, Matie, and the fawns entered the barn. "Raven has begun his search. He will give a loud call from the top of the tree nearest Kwaad if he finds him. Let's get started. Young fawns, stay on trails near a mother. Kittens, you stay in the barn in case Kwaad returns. We'll all return to the barn before nightfall."

We each took a different trail into the forest, but remained within earshot of a neighboring trail as we searched over and under its obstacles. To my right were Igo and his family. To my left were Suki and Sidekick's family. The day was shortened by the winter sun, but we spent every moment of it searching for Kwaad to no avail. The kittens rushed to the barn door in anticipation when we returned, but soon scaled the hay bales in sorrow. Suki tried her best to console them while Sidekick, Raven, Matie, and I discussed search tactics for the following day.

"We did a thorough job searching high and low in the woods today," commented Matie. "I don't know that searching it again tomorrow would do us any good."

"I agree," replied Sidekick. "Kwaad must have gone toward the meadow. Perhaps he found shelter in the old farm shack on the other side of the lea."

"I hope so," worried Raven. "That lea is a large, open area with little protection from predators. Humans are hunting now, so all of us must be especially careful tomorrow."

We agreed on another early start and disbanded for the night. As much as I disagreed with Kwaad's approach to life, I, too, was worried about him. Even though the kittens were afraid of him, they genuinely missed his presence. I found their attachment to Kwaad difficult to understand.

Unlike our quiet search along the dampened forest trails the previous day, each step in the unprotected, frosted grasslands crunched loudly the following morning, identifying our position. Not only could predators easily follow our trails, but everything in advance of us could hear us coming. Nonetheless, we continued our search.

"Listen," said Sidekick. "I think I heard something. Everyone stop for a minute."

"It's nothing," replied Raven circling overhead. "You heard the sound of snow falling through the roof of the old shack. Keep on searching."

We slowly made our way through the meadow and searched the old shack, but there was no sign of Kwaad or any other creature in the fresh snow. Disappointed, we headed back to the barn where Tess was waiting for us.

"Did you find him?" she asked Suki, as she combed the long thick coat of Jasmine.

"No, Tess," replied Suki ashamedly. "We searched the forest, meadow, and old farm shack. Where else could he be?"

Tess thought for a moment, twirled her braided hair around a finger, and responded, "With my lost balls, perhaps."

Suki gave Tess a strange look that Tess seemed to understand.

"Remember when I was little, Suki, and I would play ball outside with you? Whenever I threw the ball behind the old chicken coop by the vining maple trees, the ball would disappear. We never did find those balls."

"What is she talking about?" I asked Suki.

"She's right. I forgot all about it. She threw the ball and I would follow its trail until it disappeared under the maples. I searched until the trail ended, but never went beyond that point because the young branches mussed my coat. The trees are larger now. Let's go look!"

"Perhaps we should wait until morning when the snow won't freeze on our coats. It's dark now and we wouldn't want to lead the coyotes to Kwaad, even if we did find him," I suggested.

Before Tess returned to the house, she told the deer they could bed in the barn for the night if they didn't disturb the milk cows.

After we all snuggled in for the night, I noticed Igo staring at Mildred. "What's on your mind, Igo?"

Rather sheepishly, he replied, "I was just admiring her udder. I know I'm too old to nurse now, but Mildred seems to have a plentiful supply going to waste. What a mother load of milk!"

"It's for Tess and the humans, Igo. Just close your eyes."

When the first rays of sunlight streamed through the barn slats, our search team gathered to follow Suki to the area behind the abandoned chicken coop. Branches of the trees were laden with snow, except for the sunny side that had dropped its weight, forming a crater under the tree. I walked closer to explore the large hole and realized how much deeper it really was. As I turned to comment to the others, I heard a feeble mew that brought everyone to the edge of an abandoned cistern that was no longer covered with wooden slats. Thick moss had rotted the boards, and heavy snow had sent them plummeting to the bottom, where they were wedged just above water level. Clinging to the top board was Kwaad, cold, wet, hungry, and embarrassed, but glad to be found. Elated to find Kwaad alive, our celebration caught the attention of Tess and her father, who had begun their milking chores.

"Do you see any balls down there?" hollered Tess. We all laughed and cheered.

Once again, Suki's man came to the rescue. He tied a rope to the handle of a vegetable basket and lowered it down the cistern, where Kwaad anxiously jumped in for the ride up.

"How did you come to fall down that hole?" I asked Kwaad.

"I took a late-afternoon nap the other day and didn't wake until the snow had started falling. On my way home, I chased a rabbit that gracefully jumped over the two snowy mounds. I plunged in and fell down the hole between them. Thank you for looking for me, Topper. I didn't think you would after our argument."

"Nonsense. I should be thanking you."

"What do you mean?"

"I simply mean that I appreciate the memory."

Still not understanding the point I was trying to make, Kwaad asked Suki for a better explanation of my comment.

"Topper believes that our daily experiences provide us with memories that prevent us from looking back on a lot of empty yesterdays. Our search for you provided him with something he feels is worth remembering."

"You two cats are quite unusual."

"Oh, I don't think we're as atypical as you might think."

"Well, I've never met any cats like you."

"I imagine you haven't if you've always kept to yourself. Life is full of variety, Kwaad, if you're willing to notice it."

I glanced back at Kwaad and saw, for the first time, the quiet look of contemplation on his face; his tight muscles had relaxed a little. The concepts Suki mentioned were slowly gaining acceptance by him, like the gradual warmth from a winter sun.

Having reached the nadir of his despair after three days in the bottom of the cistern, every day thereafter seemed brighter for Kwaad. The transformation was not a quick one, but slower recognition sometimes endures future challenges better.

"You know, Kwaad, the kittens meant it when they said they loved you and were worried when you were missing. Why didn't you return their affection?" I asked.

"Because I don't love them. They aren't mine."

"But you said you loved their mother."

"That's different. I fell in love with Raba, but I never wanted a family of kittens."

"Then why did you stay with her?"

"Because I was waiting for the kittens to grow and leave home, so Raba and I could be alone and enjoy each other." He took a deep breath and said, "Even the thought of her warms my soul."

I could see that Kwaad's memory of her was still vivid and his body longed for her presence.

"Don't you think you might grow to love the kittens too, since they are a part of her?"

"No, Topper. The kittens were always on her mind, distracting her attention from me. Everything between us would have been perfect without them around."

"Raba wouldn't have changed when they were gone, Kwaad. A good mother always thinks about her offspring no matter where they are. A mother's choice always includes what is best for her offspring."

"Maybe, but kittens aren't in my plans. I want to live in the moment and not be distracted or burdened by the issues of others."

I listened to Kwaad describe the attributes he had liked about Raba and realized they were the same qualities that made her a good mother. Kwaad had a famished yearning for Raba's love, but he wasn't willing to share her love with others.

"Love is not labored. It is not a competition. It is a patiently unfolding emotion. If you had imprisoned Raba's love, it would have ceased to exist. Fire and frost don't thrive together, tomcat. It's to your advantage that your mate expressed her love for everything in her experience."

Kwaad flashed me a stern look and replied, "What you say doesn't work for me, so just leave it alone. Kittens are fine as long as they aren't my constant responsibility. I like my life to have just one focus. Like it or not, that's what I want, and I don't want to discuss it with you anymore."

Even though Kwaad didn't want to discuss it further, I continued to examine in my mind the ways in which he alienated himself from his own needs. Because he refused to use his gift to enrich the lives of others, Kwaad continued looking outside himself for happiness. This was neither good nor bad, but it obviously delayed his progress toward happiness.

"I understand. Sometimes we are our own biggest obstacle. I won't mention it again."

After a deliberate change in his mood, Kwaad stated, "I wish you well, Topper, but your approach to life isn't mine. It doesn't work for me. I think it's better if we just say good-bye and go our separate ways."

"Separate journeys aren't necessary," I pleaded, but Kwaad departed at right angles to my path.

"They are for me. Good-bye."

"Not good-bye, Kwaad, just later."

"Think of it however you want, but it's good-bye for me. I'm out of here!"

I returned to Sidekick and discussed with her my reluctance in allowing Kwaad to leave in disagreement.

"I know you, Topper. You always fluff and circle your bed in order to create a comfortable place for rest."

"What's wrong with that?"

"Nothing, as long as you aren't preparing the bed for someone else. They may prefer a harder surface for their comfort level. The difference of opinion is no reflection of guilt on you or Kwaad. You've stirred his thought and, at some point, he will find a place to put the issue to rest, as must you. Remember, he said his mother named him Kwaad because he was angry at birth. Change is sometimes a slow process."

I thanked Sidekick for listening compassionately. I hoped my path would cross Kwaad's again in the future. As much as I disagreed with his approach to life, I still admired his stalwart qualities. In his absence, I would look after Suki and the kittens. My physical stature was not as sturdily appealing as Kwaad's, but, in a challenge, my determination was equally as stubborn as his. A friend's departure can feel like a winter wind, with its empty chill, replacing a familiar presence. I missed Kwaad's presence, but not his anger, and wished him well in his search for a gentler, more accepting life contract.

With the winter winds and shorter days came less aerial activity. The paired eagles, whom we watched during their remarkable courtship ritual of locking talons and spiraling toward the ground with their wings parsing the wind, were now spending most of their time protected from the wind. Their nests on the eastern bluffs were as long as a cougar and as deep as a bobcat burrow. Even though eagles have very poor night vision, they spend the shortened daylight hours stealing rather than earning their catch. The longer they fly, the more they must eat, so it is a matter of survival rather than a moral issue for them.

With no acrobatics of aerial courtship to observe in the winter sky, Toobig and I searched under rocks in the tidal pools for entertainment provided by side-shuffling crabs. The sandy gravel of the shoreline, covered in eel and other remnant sea grasses, was often used as a nursery for the young crabs, but at low tide it exposed them to predators, such as gulls. Therefore, they hid under the rocks for protection from predators, heat, and saltless rain.

"Those crabs live way too precarious a life during their first two years," commented Toobig.

"Why do you say that?"

"During those years they have no hard shell to protect them. If they survive, their shells harden to become practically impenetrable, except during their annual molting season when they hide in the sand, waiting for a new shell to grow."

"Have you seen them without a shell?"

"Yes, unfortunately. I have firsthand knowledge of the ferociousness of crab claws."

"Were you badly hurt by a claw?" I asked.

"No. It could have been much worse. She only clipped a few contour feathers. I got too close exploring her features one day. A nip from her claws warned me to keep a respectful distance."

"Were you going to eat her?" I asked.

"No, no, no! I was simply fascinated by the arrangement of her legs. Crabs move sideways, you know. Did you also know that crabs have ten legs?" asked Toobig. "Their claws are on the two front legs, and they use them to pull food toward their mouths. And the male crab has one claw much larger than the other. Then they have six walking legs and two swimming legs. Next time you see a crab, Topper, also notice the tiny hairs on its shell."

"Why would a crab, with a coat of armor, need hair?"

"The tiny hairs detect movement in the water and warn of an approaching predator."

"They do seem to be remarkable creatures, but I think I'd rather keep my distance."

"Probably a good idea. I learned my first lesson in patience from crabs. My mother had us observe them because she said they live as slowly as they grow. I always wanted to have their ability to regrow injured body parts."

"That's awesome! If I knew how, I'd certainly like to replace my tail. I had a handsome plume until it got caught in a trap."

"Dude, that's awful! Tell me about it."

"There's no time now. I have to get back to the barn. See you later, Toobig."

In the distance, I heard the muffled sound of a ship's horn blowing repeatedly. It was customary to hear horns blow as ships entered and departed the port, but this tooting sounded more distressed. I looked back in time to see Toobig head out to sea to investigate the disturbance.

All was well when I arrived at the barn. Suki was deep in thought; the three kittens were busy at their own tasks. They were typical siblings, each with a unique attribute. Jasmine, the firstborn, looked regal in her appearance and gait. She was the poet who took time to appreciate everything in life. Jesse, with his long, awkward, skinny stature, was hesitant and suspicious of anything new to him. He clumsily explored the unknown a few paces behind his siblings. Mandu moved athletically with self-assurance and fearlessness. No challenge seemed beyond his ability to master, eventually.

"Hey, Topper, how's it going?" greeted Mandu as I entered the barn.

"Fine, just fine, Mandu. Did anything happen today while I was away?"

"Today has been awesome! We caught five mice and scared about a dozen more in the haystacks. Afterward, Jasmine and I climbed the post to the loft and played in some empty boxes up there."

"What about Jesse?"

"He couldn't make it more than halfway up the post, so he took a bath and swatted flies."

"Just you wait, Mandu. He'll be a challenge someday, as soon as his muscles catch up with his growth spurt."

"By the way, Topper, you should know that Tess and her father were in here earlier doing their milking chores, and I think something is askew. Tess left before combing us, and that is unusual for her."

"It certainly is. Did Suki say anything?"

"Not yet, but I'm sure she noticed it too."

After cleaning the ears of each kitten and nodding good night to Suki, I returned to Sidekick, Matie, and the fawns for a much-needed rest. The cold night air made my heart work harder, and mountain memories filled my thoughts.

I recalled Queenie's advice to avoid slopes of forty-five degrees or less after winter storms, because the fresh snow did not freeze immediately to the packed snow beneath it. Even the wind could cause it to easily slide off and start an avalanche.

I remembered the roar and crashing of falling trees and the way a mixture of heavy snow, rain, and wind cleared a path down the mountainside. Steeper slopes lost their fresh snow gradually as it fell, so there was less accumulation on the ice packs to produce such danger. Winter in the Northwest was usually bookended by warm chinook winds that flooded the lowlands with melting mountain snows. Even in this beautiful mountain valley of Ravenwood, danger loomed as seasons changed to maintain equilibrium. Extreme situations reminded us of how fragile life is. Not knowing how long anything would last impressed upon me the importance of respecting and appreciating each moment. I looked on the cliff above me and noticed how little soil seemed to be feeding the rocky root bed of a giant fir tree. As with everything in the forest, the tree didn't need an abundance of nutritious soil to survive. A little nutrition was enough.

The winter night air was cool, crisp, and quiet. Tonight, I would enjoy the quietness of winter, snuggled among my friends, whereas in summer months, I often bedded near a fast-flowing stream, where there were fewer insects to pester me and a pleasant rippling sound to lull me to sleep. According to Sidekick, there was a season for everything.

Black Tidings

"Get up! Get up!" croaked Raven vehemently when the sun broke through the forest. "The Black Invader is approaching the shoreline. Come with me! Come and see!"

Without taking time to stretch, we all rushed to the shoreline through the dense forest beneath Raven's wing shadow. Circling a large tanker in the harbor were small boats, towing booms and skimmers in an attempt to contain the disaster. But not even man's quick response could deter the Black Invader from riding the waves to shore.

"What is that ugly stuff?" I asked loudly, to be heard over the sounds of humans yelling and horns belching out warnings.

"It's oil. Bad, bad oil!" replied Tess as her father, carrying Tess in his arms, struggled up the rise behind us. "We heard the warning signal last night, but we were hoping the oil would be contained before it reached the estuaries and coastline." Her father, a little breathless from his effort, gently lowered Tess to the ground and massaged her injured leg. He reiterated Tess's warning.

"Stay away from it," commented her father. "It kills everything it touches."

The silence of gloom fell over us as we continued to watch the waves deposit the slick darkness at our feet.

"This is a huge catastrophe!" exclaimed Toobig. "Huge, huge, huge. My parents have seen it before. They say we must warn as many sea animals as possible to avoid the Black Invader. I'll warn the pelagic birds to go far out to sea. Topper, you must warn the river otters to go upstream beyond the estuaries. Sidekick, you and the deer find as many forest animals as possible and tell them to avoid the ocean beaches. This shoreline is no longer safe for anyone."

"How long must they stay away?" I asked Toobig.

"A long time, dude! We must stay away until the ocean current dilutes the Black or washes it away."

I remembered Toobig telling me that as few as three tidal cycles could completely exchange the water along the shoreline, whereas it might require as many as sixty cycles to exchange deeper waters. The previously white cresting tides, which I had watched advance from left to right along the shore, were now depositing black sludge everywhere before their slow retreat.

I ran quickly toward the estuary where I had met Rowdy and Rascal. It was still early morning and I hoped they had not yet approached the estuary for breakfast. With so much oil in the water, there would be little room for oxygen-infused nutrients that were vital to sea life. Now, in its ponderous, almost stagnant motion, the ocean was no longer a symbol of perpetual renewal.

"Rowdy! Rascal!" I yelled, with increasing intensity. "Rowdy! Rascal! Where are you?"

I walked along, dodging low branches and remnant silk webs from the summer orb weavers. Their sticky silk on my fine cat hair would make grooming especially difficult.

"Rowdy! Rascal!" I continued calling, "Please answer!"

"What's up, Topper? Why all the shouting?"

"I've come to warn you to stay away from the estuary and ocean. The Black Invader has covered the water and shore."

"Oh, no! The Black Invader will destroy the salmon and their food supply," exclaimed Rowdy. "The chain will be broken!"

"Calm down, dear," pleaded Rascal as she tried to comfort him. "We'll find a way to survive."

"I'm sure we will, but it's not just us I'm thinking about. The salmon migration upstream each year is important to all of us, animals and plant life!

Rowdy was right. Every fowl and beast that feeds on fish comes to the river during the spawning season. Without decaying, floating, salmon carcasses, the river bacteria wouldn't have the nutrients needed to feed the underwater plants and animals.

"Don't you understand, Rascal? This estuary will no longer be a suitable refuge for us and our friends. We will be forced to move away from our dream home."

As far as Rascal was concerned, moving was a worse fate than not eating, and so I had two otters to comfort.

"Perhaps you could move upstream, beyond the waterfall, where the Black wouldn't affect you so much," I offered. "At least you would still live along the same stream."

"No, that wouldn't work, Topper." explained Rowdy, "The stream above the waterfall is too straight. It moves too quickly. It hasn't time to collect essential nutrients from the soil."

Rowdy knew the river well. Its bed was shallow and exposed to sunlight most of the day. Not only would it hold less oxygen in the dry summer heat, but without deciduous trees nearby, there wouldn't be fallen leaves in the water to decay and provide nutrients.

"Well, at least you wouldn't be pestered by mosquitoes upstream." I teased.

"No; this meandering river estuary is the ideal home for us. Even though the slow water is a breeding ground for mosquitoes, I can tolerate a few females stealing nutrients from my blood to help their eggs develop."

"Uh-huh!" replied Rascal. "I'll remind you of that next summer when you complain about their saliva making you itch."

Having warned the otters, but not knowing how to ease their worries, I headed back to the shoreline, where Toobig was resting from having alarmed the pelagics.

"It's gonna be worse than I thought," said Toobig as he shook his head sorrowfully. "The winter transients have already arrived. There are large flocks of buffleheads, goldeneyes, ruddy ducks, and grebes along the shore, and with a moonless night approaching, they won't be able to see the Black floating toward them. I hate to think what awful sights tomorrow will bring."

I shook my head in despair and looked around me. "Hey, where's Suki? I thought she would come down with you, Tess."

"No, she didn't come down with us. Perhaps she stayed home with the kittens."

"I think I'll go back and check on her since there's nothing more for me to do here."

"See you tomorrow, Topper. Make it bright and early," said Toobig, staring into the fading sunlight.

I didn't enjoy alarming Suki with bad news, but she always took it well after the initial shock. She was amazingly open-hearted and well centered in dealing with life's challenges. Like Sidekick, very little perplexed her for long.

Upon entering the barn, I found Suki in the kitten pile with her arm around Mandu. What a wonderful mother figure! The vision enthralled me. I hoped to share a family with Suki someday soon.

"What a serene sight the four of you are!" I exclaimed tenderly.

"Thank you, Topper," whispered Suki, with a jubilant smile that encouraged me to join the sleeping pile. Just being near Suki restored my sense of equanimity. The softness of her pillowed breast, and the slow rise and fall of her chest with each mellow breath, instantly transformed my previous worries into tranquility. No greater sense of blissful contentment had I ever known. With her by my side, the world would always be hopeful.

The sun rose too soon the following morning, and I felt somewhat discombobulated. I knew Toobig was waiting for me to somehow help him with the black tragedy, but my senses didn't want to disengage from thoughts of Suki.

"You must go, Topper, and I must stay with the kittens," instructed Suki reluctantly.

I gently rose to my feet, nuzzled her once more, and let my feet lead my dazed mind toward the ocean. It wasn't that I had an aversion to helping Toobig; I simply enjoyed the enchanted emotions associated with Suki.

As I approached the shoreline, I heard Toobig's exasperated voice shouting. "Don't eat it! Don't eat it! The Black will kill you!"

The tide was out and gulls were following their routine of rounding up mollusks. Toobig dive-bombed them in a panic and forbade them to crack open the shells. Some disgruntled gulls jeered at him, some flew off apprehensively, and others, unrattled by his warning, continued fighting over the toxic food. The shoreline rocks and sand were streaked with dark slime. The tidal pools contained oil rainbows that distorted the fragile contents. Offshore, loons and cormorants were frantically preening the oil-slicked feathers that had once made them efficient divers and insulated them from the icy waters. Toobig was right. The impact of the oil spill would be huge on land and sea inhabitants.

I waved to Toobig and indicated that I would patrol the estuary and river, where animals often stopped for a refreshing drink. As I approached, I saw a family of six raccoons starting to cross the river.

"Get out! Get out!" I shouted alarmingly. "The water has been fouled."

Very obediently, the adults halted their advance and returned to shore.

"What do you mean? Why is the water dangerous?" asked the father raccoon.

"Oil has contaminated the estuaries. You may not be able to see it easily, but when the sunlight is just right, you can see the slick that floats on top. If the oil gets on your skin or you lick it, you might die."

"Then how are we supposed to get back home across the river?"

"I suggest you travel farther upstream beyond the reach of the waves and cross there."

"That's very kind of you, cat. Thank you for the warning."

"My name is Topper, and I'm glad to do it. Please warn others that you see, and tell them to spread the word too. By the way, you have a nice family. I hope to have one myself someday. Take good care of them."

"Thank you, Topper. They're a handful sometimes, but we try to do our best. Sometimes four seems like too many, but I wouldn't want to give any of them back, don't you know."

"Travel safely, and stay away from lowland waters."

"What about the salmon spawning next fall? We depend on them for most of our protein, as do the bears and other forest animals."

"I don't know when the waters will clear. Salmon are high up on the fish food chain. Even if the waters clear by fall, the salmon might have eaten smaller, contaminated fish, so that eating the salmon would pass the contamination along to you."

"Yes, I understand. Disruption anywhere in the food chain is dangerous for every species above it."

With heavy hearts, we each went our separate ways. Before heading back to the barn, I was able to warn eagles, otters, and coyotes of the potential danger. All seemed appreciative of my gesture, and even the hungry coyote decided not to take advantage of my vulnerable position. Suki would be proud of my effort and accomplishment.

I entered the barn quietly and returned to the warm spot next to Suki, which the kittens had thoughtfully left vacant for me. Satisfied with my day's work, I slept peacefully next to Suki's calm body. Before daybreak, I repositioned myself and nudged Suki a few times in hopes that she would stir. Being unsuccessful, I nuzzled closer to her and decided she must have had an energetic day with the kittens, who were also still sleeping. It wasn't long before my stomach began growling and woke the kittens. They were likewise ready for breakfast.

The clanging of the feed bucket indicated that Tess was starting her rounds. Tess was walking more easily today, and soon there would be fresh warm milk to sip, thanks to Maude and Mildred. The kittens rushed toward Tess and I began the hunt for an unfortunate rodent with which to surprise the sleeping Suki. As most of the small barn animals had become guarded since the arrival of so many kittens, my task was not an easy one. I managed to catch a forlorn shrew and took it to Suki, now awake, but a bit detached from the barn activity.

"Thank you for the shrew, Topper. May I save it for later?"

"What's bothering you, if you don't mind me asking?"

She looked up at me with a worried, depleted expression.

"I appreciate everything you've done for me. When I was stranded, you rescued me. When I was hungry, you fed me. When I was lonely, you comforted me. When I was sad, you delighted me. When I was confused, you inspired me. When I was dismayed, you invigorated me."

"And now? What are you feeling now?"

"I'm feeling … umm … I think I'm feeling anguished."

"What is paining you? What can I do to help?"

"Just trust me, Topper. Trust that what I tell you is true."

"I do trust you. I always have. I don't doubt you at all."

"Then that is enough. We'll talk more later. Mandu needs you to teach him how to climb the rope to the top of the loft window. He wants to chase pigeons up there."

"I'll teach him, but can't it wait until after we finish our discussion?"

"No. Some things can't wait. Do it now, please."

Obediently, I called Mandu over to the thick, dangling rope and began his shimmy lesson. It took several attempts before he made it to the top, but once he did, I knew no pigeon would ever be safe up there again. A little encouragement went a long way with Mandu, a cat with more confidence than most. He stood proudly at the highest point in the barn and then began prancing, flipping, and singing.

"Oh, yes. Oh, yes. Uh-huh … uh-huh … uh-huh!"

Impressed by his passion for success, I decided Mandu needed no more encouragement from me. I headed out the door to meet Toobig.

"Topper, may I talk to you?" inquired Tess, approaching the barn with a pitchfork.

"Certainly. What may I do for you?"

"I want to talk to you about Suki. I'm concerned about her not eating. She's always had a healthy appetite, but lately she refuses to eat her food and salmon treats. She seems thirsty all the time, standing over her bowl, but won't drink the milk or water that I offer."

"Not even salmon? I thought she was tired of the shrews I brought her and was just being polite."

"No. She hasn't been eating or drinking anything for a week now and has lost a great deal of strength and weight."

I had been gone during the days since the oil spill and was unaware of the changes in Suki, since I only slept next to her at night. Perhaps not eating was what made her feel anguished.

"I'll have a talk with her this evening when I return. Hasn't she said anything to you?"

"She only says she loves me and is grateful for the times we've shared together. I need her love, Topper, but the amount of time she spends in my lap nuzzling under my chin frightens me now. I don't know what she needs me to do."

Tears were rolling down each red cheek of Tess's face. She tightened her lips and squinted her bloodshot eyes. "I love her so much. I can't stand to lose her. Suki has always been here to listen to my troubles. She calms me and shows me a better way of thinking. I'll be lost without her!"

I knew exactly how Tess felt. Suki was all that and more to me. I gave Tess a reassuring wink and walked through her legs in a figure-eight motion.

"Suki would never leave you alone, Tess. You are equally important to her. Trust her."

As the last two words left my lips, I remembered Suki's command that morning. *Trust that what I tell you is true!*

My day with Toobig was the beginning of a devastating education in the acute and chronic effects of crude oil on the habitats and animals in a winter marine environment. In the shallow tidal flats were carcasses of shovelers, scaups, scoters, buffleheads, mergansers, and loons, and the large bodies of blue herons, whose oil-covered bodies were no longer buoyant, insulated, or capable of flying. Plovers and sanderlings were stuck in large globules of oil on the beach, easy targets for raptors who didn't realize eating that prey might be their last suppers.

"What a tragedy!" I exclaimed.

"Yes, but it's only just begun." Toobig sighed. "Dude, what we see here are only the direct effects of hydrocarbons on the bodies of marine life. The devastation continues where we can't see it now."

"What do you mean?"

"The damage isn't just external, Topper. There is internal damage also."

I contemplated how oil could get inside animals and realized it could be ingested through their instinctive preening of feathers and fur. The ingested oil would affect so much of the animal's body that it would die.

"Toobig," I asked sorrowfully, "are they all going to die straight away?"

"No. Some will live for a while before they die. The oil weakens their bodies, so that they won't be able to fight off infections to stay healthy."

"This is horrible. What you describe is painful and long lasting."

"Absolutely, dude. It can affect many generations. My parents said the loss of marine prey due to the pollution will force animals who are higher on the food chain to abandon their homes or travel farther for food. Some may even have to change their food choices due to a scarcity of what they normally eat. Moving or changing their food choices will mean more animals fighting others for less food in smaller, congested areas. There's no happy ending to this story."

"If they move or change their diet, can't they survive?"

"Not necessarily. Having to work so hard and travel so far for less food will lower their body mass. If they are too skinny or their nutrition too poor, their offspring will get progressively weaker too. Entire species could be wiped out in only a few generations!"

Disturbed by all that Toobig was saying, I searched the shoreline for survivors and saw a yearling gull preening one wing that had been dipped in oil.

"Look. Surely that young gull will survive," I said hopefully. "Only one wing is oiled."

"Perhaps, but you must realize that the more time he spends preening, the less time he has to search for food. If he ingests any of the oil he preens from his feathers, it will affect his gut."

I knew what would happen if the gut absorbed the oil. The bird, like other animals, would become more dehydrated and, with so much oil lining its gut, food nutrients wouldn't get absorbed.

"It's so sad, so pointless," I moaned. "Life will never be the same, even for the survivors!"

I followed Toobig along the high tide line, observing the misery around me. Hypothermic, dehydrated, and anemic birds were frantically struggling against their adversity. On a sea stack offshore, I could see a family of seals trying to clean their fur and protect their thermoregulators.

"What will the whales do about the oil?" I asked.

"They're affected a bit differently," he responded. "Cetaceans depend on blubber for insulation, so the oil doesn't affect their core temperature as it does in birds, otters, and fur seals. Consuming oil-contaminated food, however, can cause failure of internal organs in whales, just as it does in other species."

"What can we do to help these animals if we must also avoid the oil?"

"Unfortunately, Topper, my parents said there's not much we can do for an animal once it's been oiled. Our job is to warn others of the tragedy and hope they avoid contact with anything in the food chain that might have been affected."

I looked closely at Toobig's face and realized that the oil spill would change our lives too. No longer could we hunt clams together during low tides. Toobig would have to leave this shoreline to find food elsewhere.

"When and where will you go, Toobig?"

"Tomorrow, dude. I'll leave with my family and head farther down the coast where the oil hasn't contaminated the shore. I'll miss you, Topper. You've been a great pal!"

"I'll miss you too, and the delicacy of clam feasts! Perhaps you can send word with Raven when you find a new home. Surely we will meet again sometime."

"I hope so. Please give my well wishes to Suki, Sidekick, and the rest of your family. I'm glad to know you'll be in a good situation. Later, dude!"

"Absolutely! Later."

The walk back to the barn was gloomy. No longer could I hunt with Toobig. No longer could the fawns play in the tidal pools. More things than I could imagine would change. I was glad Sidekick had taught me to notice everything, because one never knew how long anything will last.

My thoughts drifted back to Tess's concern for Suki. I felt ashamed for not having spent more time with Suki. In retrospect, I realized that I hadn't seen Suki eat or drink. Because her beautiful fur was so long, at first glance her appearance hadn't seemed to change much. However, I had noticed that her rib cage and spine were protruding more prominently when I cuddled next to her. As Suki was not one to complain, I decided I would have to ask her straight out what was happening to her.

"Suki, are you feeling well?" I whispered as I snuggled next to her in the barn.

"No. My body doesn't seem to be processing food anymore, and I'm very weak."

"I'm so sorry that I didn't notice earlier. I just thought you were tired from looking after the kittens by the time I returned each day. What can I do for you?"

"Just cuddle with me, Topper. You've already done everything else. All I need is you."

"You've always had me. From the moment I first laid eyes on you clinging to the log in the river, I was impressed with you. You are everything I ever wanted in my life. You are hopeful, compassionate, and calm, even while cascading down the river on a log! I've always been yours, Suki, totally and completely."

"I know," responded Suki in a giddy fashion. "I saw the admiration in your eyes when you rescued me from the river. I heard the compassion in your voice whenever you spoke to me. I tasted the yearning in your tears when you were sad. I smelled the pleasure in your saliva whenever you licked my face. But most of all, I felt your ever-present love, even when you were away."

"I'm so glad that you felt what I felt."

Suki leaned against my chest as I wrapped my arms around her and licked her ears. All night long we held each other and recalled our adventures together. At times we laughed, but always our hearts were cherishing the shared moments that had enriched our lives.

"I'm so grateful that we have these memories forever."

"Forever isn't long enough, Topper. We must love each other longer than forever. Love must outlast everything else."

I heard the nostalgia in her voice fade into sadness as she closed her eyes. Only faintly now could I hear the purr of air passing her hyoid and voice folds. Very slowly, now, she inhaled and exhaled. I hoped the endorphins her purrs released would ease her pain. I slowly licked her face and cleaned her ears until a cold fear rushed into my aching heart. The soothing rumble stopped.

"No, Suki, don't you leave me. I need you! Please, please, I need you in my life."

My entire body shook in desperation. I would do anything, anything at all, to keep her with me.

"Love longer, Topper," whispered Suki feebly.

"If forever is not long enough, then … I shall love you … forever and a day."

A serene glow sparkled in her eyes and she said, "Yes, forever and a day is long enough. Let me go now, and trust me when I say you will meet another companion to love. And when you do, love her as you've loved me."

I held Suki's dark velvet head against my trembling chest and looked into her glazed blue eyes. Never again would there be a cat like Suki, at least not for Tess or me. I gently released my hold on Suki's limp body and watched the sorrowful kittens lick her paws and face. Very slowly I approached the house to tell Tess and try to comfort her.

The Promise

As much as love feels good in secure times, it hurts equally as much when love seems absent. The pain of lost love is so agonizing that one is tempted never to love again. The loss, the emptiness weighs heavily on the bereaved, conjuring dark emotions that are eased by the support of friends and the realization of a new expression of love.

For three days after Suki left, I moped around the forest with Sidekick and her fawn. So much had changed in my life in such a short time that dealing with every emotion was difficult for me. The grief that I felt for the loss of Suki was exacerbated when I realized that I was still grieving for my human, Maggie, and the loss of my previous life. My heart was heavy with such an ache and emptiness that I wondered if I could ever feel at ease again.

"How are you feeling today?" inquired Sidekick.

"I don't seem to feel anything," I replied. "I'm emotionally numb."

"Is there anything I can do to help relieve you of the pain you are experiencing?"

"I don't know, Sidekick. I'm glad Suki is no longer in pain, but I miss her terribly. And I understand why Toobig had to leave. I know he will do fine in his new home, but something is keeping me from being happy for him. I want to be happy, but this terrible emptiness is all I feel. I'm trying to get rid of the wistful loneliness, but, for the first time in my life, sorrow seems to be overpowering the joy in me."

Before Sidekick could respond, Iya interrupted.

"Come here, Momma! What is this baby twig going to be?" Iya asked, poking her hoof at a small stick in the ground.

Iya was now only slightly shorter than Sidekick, but still as curious as a younger, wide-eyed fawn. Iya examined every new hoof and paw print, sniffed odd-shaped fungi, and jumped whenever the wind dislodged snow from the cedar branches.

"What was it before, dear?" Sidekick encouraged her and approached Iya slowly. "What plant dropped its seed there, do you think?"

Iya looked around and above her with spellbound brown eyes. Nothing ceased to amaze her. Her innocent curiosity was a constant stimulus, and I was about to learn another lesson from her curiosity.

"Uh, well, uh, I think those bare trees overhead are alders, so I guess this twig will grow to be an alder too."

"Absolutely, Iya. That's the most likely possibility! We shouldn't be surprised by what grows when we know what seed has been planted."

Sidekick glanced in my direction and tugged on the greenery that had brushed her tall ear. I returned a nod in her direction to indicate that I had learned the lesson too. If I wanted to experience a change in my attitude, I would have to prepare the soil of my thoughts to welcome a more desirable seed.

It was good to spend time with my deer friends. Ours was a comfortable relationship that required very little explanation most of the time. When I wasn't hunting, I spent long hours lounging under the cover of cedars. Every few days I visited the barn kittens and comforted Tess. She hugged each kitten tightly, almost afraid to release it, so I made it a point to distract her attention periodically before the captive kitten became too overheated.

One rainy morning I rushed for shelter in the barn and discovered a new visitor standing in the doorway. She introduced herself as Kiisu. Similar to Suki, she was a young Himalayan with blue eyes, a light-colored coat, and a faint blue-gray shading on her face, ears, and paws. I examined her closely with much reservation. Her eyes were blue, but they were not enchanting like Suki's. Her coat was long, but it was not silken like Suki's. Her face was dark, but it was not velvet like Suki's.

As much as my heart wanted to remain reserved and apprehensive, I was awed by the physical similarity to Suki, and inspired to be amused again. The kittens kept close watch on my expressions while I inquired about the travels that had brought Kiisu here. In a timid but delightful voice, Kiisu explained that she had been born a runt and abandoned by her mother in order that her siblings would have enough food.

"I've been learning on my own how to survive," Kiisu explained, "but I still have much to experience."

Kiisu looked at each of us and wiped a damp paw across her face.

"I've tried to keep my fur clean and in place, but no matter how much I lick it, it always dries in a disheveled fluff like this."

Kiisu turned her head and rubbed behind her ears. I simply couldn't contain my laughter any longer. Her expression was as forlorn as her fur was mussed, making a spiked halo around her wide blue eyes.

"Yep," I said, "you are definitely having a bad fur day! Is there anything we could do to help?"

My jovial comment could have been exactly the wrong thing to say to a young female in distress, but Kiisu joined in the laughter, to the relief of us all.

"May I stay with you in the barn? That is, if you think there's room for me."

The fact that she asked permission to stay was a welcome gesture and showed that she took nothing for granted. She was a cat who would be appreciative of what our friendship could offer her.

"I'm s-s-sure we'd all enjoy having you join us," stuttered Mandu, looking toward me for accord.

"Yes," I agreed. "You are welcome to share our supplies and adventures."

"Oh my, adventures sound exciting. Where may I bed?"

Most cats fought to claim the highest resting place with a broad view and little exposure, but Kiisu would be content with whatever she received.

I looked at Mandu expectantly. "Mandu will lead you to the hay bale between him and Jesse. She will be safe there, won't she, Mandu?"

"You bet, Topper. I'll make sure of it."

As Mandu led Kiisu to the proper hay bale, I heard him explain to her the parameters of safety and our daily routine. With Mandu as her guide, Kiisu was bound to experience adventure soon.

My eyes followed her graceful ascent that again reminded me of Suki. As similar as she was to Suki, my emotion for her was not the same. My love for Suki would never end, but would continue to be a work in progress. For now, however, I was grateful that Kiisu's arrival had rescued my eyes from tears.

Two thousand seabirds were oiled by the Black Invader, according to Raven's report, and it was unknown how many other animals would eventually be indirectly affected and suffer related chronic illnesses. So many lives in the great Northwest depend on its clean waters. The food chain here was a long one that included many species and habitats.

"The spilled oil is a known and visible danger to us," reminded Sidekick, "but we know very little about the toxic effects of the cleanup solutions used by man. Before he left, Toobig warned us that the dispersing solutions cannot be seen, so we must avoid all local recycled waters."

"All waters, Momma? But then where will we drink?" asked Iya.

"We must drink from the pond upriver, beyond the tidal flow in the estuaries. We must not consume the grasses along the coastal shore either. Do you understand, Iya? No longer may you play in the tidal flats."

"I understand, Momma, but how do you know all these things? How do I learn this knowledge?"

"All you need to know, Iya, exists in a blade of grass. Study it."

"How will I know when I've learned it, Momma?"

"Eternity is etched on the bottom of your hoof, dear Iya."

As Iya examined the lines on her hoof, I recalled Sidekick's advice for me to learn what exists beyond the obvious. I knew Iya wouldn't understand what her mother meant now, but time would afford her the needed perspective if she could remember her mother's words of today. With infinity available within the grasp of my paw, I would always have more to ponder.

The skies were quieter after the relocation of so many gull families. No longer could we hear the loud announcements and arguments whenever one of them discovered a treasure. I missed the excitement and exercise I got trying to guard Toobig's catch. I hadn't realized how active I had been with Toobig. Now, my daily panting up the hill to the barn was an indication that I needed a more active routine.

"One, two, three, go!" I shouted and dashed through the snow mounds, jumped four times my height up a decaying hemlock, and climbed to its only remaining branch.

"What are you chasing?" asked Sidekick, searching the empty tree for prey.

"Oh, I just thought I'd exercise my body instead of my mind for a while."

"Why have you given up on your mind?"

"I haven't given up," I said, descending the tree in reverse. "I'm just giving it a rest."

"Why is that?"

"I've been thinking too much, and it tends to drive friends away."

"Are you referring to Kwaad's departure?"

"Well, he's a good example. No matter how hard I tried to explain my thoughts to him, my ideas seemed to chase him away."

"I don't think it was as much your ideas, Topper, as it was your approach."

"I know I seemed adamant when I talked to him, but really, the raised volume of my voice was actually excitement. I enjoyed our disagreements. It's boring to always agree. I like the challenge of different concepts."

"That's all good and fun, but you need to practice fusing compassion with your wisdom. It's great that thinking excites you, but you must also have a receptive mind. If you don't, your ideas will appear threatening and friends will retreat."

"I hope I didn't blow my chance with Kwaad. What do you think I should do, Sidekick?"

"What do I think? You're asking me for moonbeams when what you need is sunlight."

"Huh?"

"Moonbeams provide light, but they cannot melt the snow. If you want an answer, then look for clarity in the sunbeam, where you can see beyond the obvious."

I left Sidekick and contemplated the power of the sunlight. When I returned to the barn, the kittens were exploring a box of remnants that Tess had stored in the loft. Jasmine had managed to remove the lid, and she and Mandu were selecting toys for entertainment. Jasmine removed a long strand of leather that was weighted with a curved needle (for repairing harness leads) and dangled it down the ladder to taunt Jesse. In his awkward manner, Jesse jumped and twisted on the barn floor in an attempt to swat at the shiny object. When those first attempts were unsuccessful, Jesse climbed a few rungs of the ladder, held tightly with his left paw, and swatted at the string of leather until he pulled it from Jasmine's paw and became entangled in it, narrowly missing the needle.

While Jesse tried to free himself, Mandu pushed a yellow ping-pong ball off the loft; its landing abruptly startled Kiisu from her nap. Barn life was never the same after the contents of the box had been exposed. As small as she was, Kiisu was amazingly agile, and very adept at keeping the ball in motion, batting it across the barn floor, through, over, around, or under every obstacle in its path.

Kiisu's talents weren't limited to playing ball either. She quickly discovered her musical talents when she joined Mandu in the loft and rummaged through the large box herself. Leaning against the side of the box and wrapped in a cloth was an old balalaika that Tess's mother had played when she was young. With his teeth, Mandu removed the cloth from the triangular instrument, and Kiisu gently plucked the three metal strings with her claws. So gentle was her touch that one hardly noticed how poorly the instrument was tuned or recognized the melody Kiisu played!

There was no rest for anyone that day until Mandu and Kiisu curled up for a nap. The previously precocious Mandu had become an attentive escort once Kiisu arrived. According to Tess, Kiisu was an irresistible force that required kissing and cuddling at every possible opportunity. This was a trait that Tess thought Kiisu shared with Suki. I don't think Kiisu was necessarily in agreement with this, because she often asked to be released. Although Kiisu did not have all of Suki's patience and other wonderful traits, there was still much to love about her. Suki's admonition to love another as I loved her was a constant reminder to me that love is never lost or wasted when it is honestly given.

In winter, the marbled gray and white bark of the deciduous alder provided a stark contrast to the otherwise monochromatic beauty of the prolific, giant evergreens, whose pungent aroma freshened every cloudy day. On one particular day, as the mountain valley renewed, refreshed, and revitalized itself, I once again struggled to remove sticky web silk from my fur. I recalled once before cursing crafty spiders and their exquisite creations, and Sidekick's subsequent sermon on perseverance.

"You curse the spiders," began Sidekick, "but they have much to teach you. They build new webs each day from scratch. They consume the web remnants from the previous day and spin a new one in a shady area where they are likely to catch unsuspecting insects. Each time a strand breaks, it is tirelessly replaced."

"Sidekick?" I inquired. "Why don't spiders get stuck in their own webs?"

"Silly cat," she said amused, "Their legs are coated with oil. The spider waits on a nonsticky radial line of the web. When a victim lands, the web silk vibrates and alerts the sleeping spider of its catch."

"Can't they build the webs someplace where I won't run through them? It would make life easier for both of us."

"They have to build their webs in shady areas or in rainforests where dew can adorn the strands, because they are easily dehydrated in the sun. You should take time to notice them. After all, their lifespans are very brief."

Sidekick continued to explain that, like the salmon, the lives of some spiders end tragically after the eggs are laid. The survival of the thousands of young spiders born each spring is totally dependent upon the mother's wisdom in choosing a protected area for the silken sac of eggs.

Sidekick was correct. There was much to admire about spiders, and as soon as I finished bathing, I would start appreciating them more.

From the first day I met Sidekick, she taught me to recognize and appreciate the jewels of life in Ravenwood. I walked the forests with her, noticing how shafts of sunlight highlighted uncurling fronds, snail trails, misty auras, and other new life that had previously gone unnoticed by me. I realized it was time for me to highlight everything around me, to appreciate all the jewels of my life. In the past, discovering something new and good had salved painful moments. The past transformed a personal crisis into an opportunity. Perhaps now, understanding the hidden secrets of what others cherish might provide a future remedy and an endless comfort.

I stood silently and observed the wilderness. The rich scent of cedar heartwood drew my attention to a bouncing branch where Raven was shadowboxing with unabated energy. Above him, clouds loomed in ominous stillness, indicating an approaching change. For the first time,

I noticed a graveyard of broken trees that had been killed by insects. An extraordinarily warm winter had prompted increased insect reproduction rates. The mountains and valleys were changing too. The glaciers were melting, causing some riverbeds to flood. Lakes, which had once been deep and refreshing, were now quickly evaporating because they no longer froze during the winter. Abruptly, a thunderous roar alerted every animal in the forest. Birds immediately took wing. I scouted for a place to hide. Then I heard an even more disturbing sound.

"No-ooo-ooo!" echoed the terrifying scream of Iya. "No, no, no!"

"Raven!" I yelled. "Where is Iya?"

Raven circled overhead a few times and pointed to a deep forest area. I ran swiftly to Iya's location. From a distance, I could faintly see Iya and she appeared to be unharmed. Breathlessly I shouted, "I'm coming, Iya!" Raven landed next to Iya and then took off again.

"Topper," he called back to me. "I'm going to locate Matie and the fawns. You stay here with Iya!"

I nodded in agreement. Finally, I saw the reason for Iya's scream. Lying on the ground beneath the cedar, legs curled around Iya, was Sidekick's flailing body.

"What happened, Iya?"

"She's been shot, Topper! A man in a large white and orange truck shot her from the truck window and then drove away. Why, Topper? Why would the man shoot her and leave?"

I was enraged that Sidekick had been shot, but I couldn't pause to understand why. My only concern was to ease Sidekick's restless pain.

"What can I do, dear friend? Tell me, what should I do?"

I was frantic and felt helpless. My mind was numb with fear and anger. Still the sound of Iya's scream reverberated in my ears and stabbed my heart.

"Calm down, Topper, and tell me what you see," came Sidekick's familiar request.

I tried to wipe away my tears with the back of my paw, but it was useless. Tears continued to fall even faster. With blurry, reddened eyes, I looked down at Sidekick's peaceful face.

"I see my dearest friend."

"Where do you see her?" continued Sidekick.

"I see her where she has always been, next to me."

"Look deeper, Topper. Don't let Iya believe what her eyes first tell her."

I motioned to Iya to move closer to me, where we both could look deeply into her mother's limpid brown eyes.

"I see the world that I love, Sidekick, surrounding you in its beauty."

"Me too, Momma!" cried Iya. "Your eyes, and all they reflect, are beautiful!"

"Where do the two of you see the beauty?"

"Deep in your eyes, Momma."

By now, Sidekick had stopped shaking. I hoped her pain was easing as she calmly focused on her family.

"Look deeper, Iya. Think deeper, Topper. What do you see?"

I swallowed with great difficulty, choking back tears that burned my throat.

"I see the love of my mentor and friend."

I turned to Iya, overcome by fear, and I licked the long jawbone of her face.

"*Where* do you see the love?"

"I see it in every aspect of your eyes. Even through the diffusion of my tears, I can see the effulgent sparkle that has always graced you, Sidekick."

Sidekick's every breath was shallow and her speech labored as she struggled to keep her eyes open to finish our lesson.

"Keep looking, Topper, until you are able to see what you believe."

Her large eyelids looked heavy, and I knew, as hard as she was struggling to keep them open, she couldn't continue much longer. I had to take a long, hard look this time. In the background of her eyes was the reflection of the evergreen forest, with Raven perched on an overlooking branch and Matie's family standing near. In the foreground was my own reflection, perfect in outline and features. I looked deeper yet into the eyes of my own reflection in hers. Perfectly positioned in the center of her eye was the reflection of my eye as we both shared one eye sparkle. One sparkle of light existing simultaneously in her eye and mine.

"I see love, Sidekick; your love, real love."

"And where do you see it, dear Topper?"

"I see it in my reflection."

"And that is where love has always been. You've spent your life looking for it, yet you have never been without it. That kind of love satisfies every need. It cannot be explained by a hundred thousand synonyms, because *love* defines the moment."

Sidekick's voice was peaceful and confident now.

"Love has many attributes, Topper, which include grace, honesty, compassion, and everything good in your life; but *love is one*. It is the emotion of the infinite, the beauty of an aftersmile."

I leaned gently against Sidekick's body and licked her face.

"I love you, Sidekick. Thank you for all the lessons."

"I love all of you too. You are my family—Iya, Topper, Matie, and of course Raven. You have been good friends. Now, live what you believe and grow in love's grace!"

"What should I do, Momma?" cried Iya.

"My dear Iya, there's only one response adequate for all questions. Love more."

As a single tear fell from her joyous eye, Sidekick rested her weary head on her shoulder and slowly took a final breath. Streams of tears rolled down the faces of the friends who circled her. Her leaving would be difficult for each of us, but, as her family, we would do our best to teach Iya and others the lessons Sidekick had taught us.

I looked at Iya to reassure her that she would always be comforted.

"I know," said Iya. "Momma said I will always have what I need, but I don't know how it is possible."

"I know it is difficult, Iya, but for now it is enough to remember it. In time, when you need it most, its meaning will become clear."

I walked one last time around Sidekick's body, dragging my feet to draw a circle around her under the moonlit sky. The love she had taught us resided not only in the outward expressions of her compassion, joy, and honesty; it was communicated through the emotion of her eye sparkle.

As the family respectfully withdrew from Sidekick's final resting place, I sat on a fallen log and looked at her once more, lying gracefully in the moonbeam. The memory of her love brought a smile to my face. I trusted in her promise that tomorrow's sunlight would clear away any doubts and someday reveal to me a fifth season.

As we refashioned our forest life, in the days and weeks that followed Sidekick's death, I realized that she had been more to me than a mother, mentor, and friend. She was the embodiment of everything good and true in my life. Her lessons were guidelines, leading me to future memories I would cherish. As difficult as some concepts were to accept initially, each lesson she had taught was pragmatic, promising a life worth remembering. She asked only that we lived what we believed. No longer would I allow the world unknown to make me fearful. The greatest loss that I feared had brought me the greatest sense of peace I'd ever known.

Before this fifth season of my life, I had worried about the future, complained about the past. I had spent days mourning the seeming loss of my mother, siblings, Maggie, Ravenwood, Tanner, Toobig, Suki, and Sidekick, feeling somehow that I had lost part of myself too as each one departed my life. But anything I had lost was due to my limited understanding, because love never left me. It was still where it had always been, inside me. All I had to do was reflect outwardly the emotion that graced me inwardly. In so doing, I would always be in the moment of love.

My life changed for the better after meeting Sidekick. Of course, there were still challenges to meet. Sidekick never guaranteed a life without conflict, but she did promise a fifth season in life that would emerge gently, providing comfort and relief.

I've lived each day guided by Sidekick's gentle truth. Although the mountain and valley lands changed as more humans made Ravenwood their home, I've remained in my lower valley home with Matie, Raven, Tess, the fawns, and the kittens. We welcome all newcomers who appreciate the treasures that Ravenwood's emerald magic offers. If you decide to join us, you too will discover the honest joy and assurance that perfect loving brings. Welcome to my aftersmile.

Love, forever and a day,
Topper

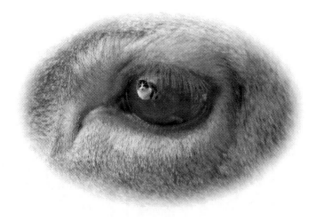

Epilogue

A t the conclusion of the stories of his journey, Topper sat at my feet in quiet reflection. I thought I saw small tears gathering under each eyelid. He raised a paw to wash his face, as if to hide his emotional release at the end of his saga. We sat together, each in deep thought, and I realized that the end of his story was not a conclusion to Topper's journey, nor to mine.

The animals of Ravenwood lived a parable of life: its cycles, its trials, and its beauty. They lived by rules for the common good, always looking forward, with yesterday's memories as the basis of hope for the good awaiting them. Their way of life, embodied in the teachings of Sidekick, revealed that self is not dependent on place nor other beings, but on what one values in life.

"Yes!" I said out loud, as much to myself as to Topper, "Ravenwood is a way of life that graces us with an aftersmile! Thank you, Topper!"

I held him in my arms and hugged his bunny-soft body. His purr was calm, his features fragile, and I could see my own reflection in his eye sparkle.